TRUE LOVE CANNOT BE MEASURED

LOVE STORY OF A CANCER SURVIVOR

POMPI MAZUMDAR

TRUE LOVE CANNOT BE MEASURED

By

Pompi Mazumdar

(Edited by Dhivya Balaji)

Copyright Information

Book description

'True Love Cannot Be Measured' is a story of love, passion, tragedy, separation, faith and bonding. The story starts with the love of a young boy and a girl who were happily married to each other and leading a contended prestigious life along with their child and their parents. One day they meet with a tragedy that brings them to the door of death. Their life was shattered into pieces with misunderstanding which led to the separation of two beautiful souls – one battling with the disease of life and death and the other having disappeared and lost with no sign of return.

Can these two beautiful hearts see the light of life again and get reunited with their families or are they lost forever? To unlock the mystery of Surojit and Avantika's (Binita's) love story, read this novel.

Dedication

I dedicate this book to

My parents, Mr Pijush Mazumdar & Mrs Manju Mazumdar

Grandparents (paternal) Late Mr Prasanna Nath Mazumdar & Late Mrs Gyanobala Nath Mazumdar; (maternal) Late Mr Kshirodh Ch. Nath & Mrs Sufala Nath

"God is the Creator of this Universe. We are the children of God. Our Parents are our Creators. Hence, our Parents are God. So, we should always worship our Parents. We are here in this universe because they brought us here. Whatever we are today is only because of them. So, we should always value them, respect them and worship them."

Pompi Mazumdar

My father and my grandfather always used a proverb, one that became one of my favourite quotes and has inspired me to be ambitious since my childhood.

"Uccho dikhey lokkho rakhiya charibey ek tir

Vidhiley Vidhitey parey himalayer sheer"

("Always aim high and release the arrow of your goals towards the topmost height. It might pierce everything and take you even far beyond the highest peaks of the mountains.")

Always dream big to fly high.

Table of Contents

Acknowledgements

I would like to thank all the situations that led me to take up writing. As people, I have noticed that most of us keep complaining to God about our small problems, always seeking His intervention in finding our solutions.

I believe that God patiently listens to us and never responds to our questions on time according to our wishes because He is the only one who understands that there is a time for everything.

He prepares us in His own manner to face our circumstances and the odds in our lives. While the process, to us, may make it seem like we are struggling and failing, I believe that we are all only learning and finally finding solutions to all our questions and unresolved situations.

In my life too, there have been many ups and downs, and I kept looking for someone to blame those failures on—people and situations that may have not necessarily wanted to harm me or bring me pain. Of late, though, I have realised that whatever happens, happens for our wellbeing.

Of course, I talk for myself when I state that had challenging situations not been a part of my life, I would not have been who I am today, a writer and an author.

I would like to thank God for giving me a beautiful son whose arrival gave birth to a new me and changed my entire world, for the birth of my son brought a new identity and meaning to my life.

I would like to thank all my friends, family members, colleagues, my networks, and the entire JobsForHer.Com team who always encouraged me to take up writing and appreciated my writings.

I would like to thank my husband Aniruddha Sarkar who always helped me with all the resources and opportunities I needed to grow and helped me embrace the process of reading, writing, learning, and exploring.

I would also like to thank Wordpress.com, Linkedin.com, and Facebook.com for giving me the platforms and opportunities to showcase my skills and talents and helped me reach out to millions of readers and customers across the globe.

Last but not least, I would like to say SPECIAL THANKS to my dear friends Sangita Kumari Rath and Debasis Sahu from Bangalore, who always supported and encouraged me and appreciated my skills and stood by me through thick and thin, and especially throughout the entire process of the publication of my first book.

Roshni Roy, my neighbour from Bangalore, you are my inspiration. You came into my life as an angel and blessed me with your magical stick of wisdom. Lots of love, thanks, and wishes to you.

"Every single person and situation whether good, bad, positive, negative, evil, the divine is connected to us for a beautiful reason."

&

"God always has something good in store for all of us."

Pompi Mazumdar

Chapter 1

Avantika Bannerjee (Binita) was a young woman from a very respected family. She was an MBA student pursuing her degree from the University of Kolkata. Her father, Hrishikesh Bannerjee, was the principal of the college. It was his last day at college and he was delivering a farewell speech.

"I thank you all for allowing me to serve in this college for 35 long years as your teacher and your colleague. It helped me build some great memories here for the rest of my life. Wishing you all good luck and good faith in whatever you do. Do take care of yourself and each other. Goodbye."

He received a huge round of applause.

Mr Hrishikesh Bannerjee had served in the mathematics department of the college for 35 long years. His wife, Mrs Arunima Bannerjee, was a bank manager. She had a few years left to serve before retirement. She returned home early that day as it was her husband's last day at work and he might feel melancholic. She came early to cook a good dinner for him before he arrived home.

Binita was a beautiful young lady who was also equally intelligent and ambitious. She was her class topper. She had a disciplined life.

Unlike girls from some other rich families, she never smoked, drank or had any kind of vices or bad company. She was also not a party animal. She mostly liked to spend time with family or study. She was very simple yet stylish. She remained busy with her studies all the time.

Binita's friend often told her, "Your life is already set and destined after completion of your MBA degree. You are intelligent, smart and beautiful and you would bag a job wherever you wish. Only mediocre students like us will face problems. It would be difficult for us to get a job in this competitive world."

Some other friends also used to tell her, "You would receive marriage proposals from all handsome and intelligent guys."

But Binita always ignored their comments with a big smile and with the words, "I would never be ready for marriage until I become independent and have a job in hand."

Her friend replied, "You just see! Someday, you will suddenly meet someone and forget all your promises. Your heart and mind would become restless and eager to get married to the man of your heart. Love is such a divine feeling, and anyone who faces it could never ignore it."

Binita sidestepped, saying, "Leave all those topics now. Let time answer you."

Binita was the only daughter of her parents, who brought her up with great love and care.

Every day, when they returned from their work, they would always sit together to have dinner as a family, followed by gossip and discussions on various topics from the day. Binita also enjoyed throwing the usual childlike tantrums with her parents.

One day, at the dinner table, her father broke the news to her mother that one of his childhood friends, Mr Omolendu Basu, a former head of FCI from Delhi, recently retired and they were relocating to Kolkata with their family. They are also looking for a bride for their son. His son had completed his Engineering from IIT Delhi and gotten an MBA from IIM Bangalore. He was posted in Kolkata. So, they were all relocating to get reunited with their family members back in their hometown.

Mr Banerjee suggested that they could all be invited to their house for lunch someday for an introduction of their children to each other. Binita then told her father that she did not want to get married right then because she was not yet ready for marriage until she had a job in her hand.

Her father replied, "What's the harm in meeting the family once? Maybe you won't like him and the question of marriage itself will be out of consideration. Isn't it?"

On hearing this, Binita agreed to the meeting.

The day arrived. Everyone was excited to meet the new family. Mr Hrishikesh Bannerjee was impatient to meet his childhood friend after a long time.

As soon as they got out of the car, Mr Bannerjee gave a big hug to Mr Basu and their joy knew no bounds. Both the wives were also happy to see and greet each other. Surojit was standing beside them with a smiling face. The family was welcomed inside the house and made themselves comfortable. Then Mrs Basu handed over some gifts that they had brought for the occasion.

Mr and Mrs Bannerjee accepted them but mentioned, "Why must you be bringing gifts? There is no room for formality in our relationship. You all could have come empty-handed."

Arunima brought in some water and juice for them in a tray and served them. Mr Omolendu introduced his son to Mr and Mrs Bannerjee.

Surojit was a tall, handsome and smart guy. He also had a special quality of convincing others with his well-behaved nature and polite behaviour. He could mingle with anyone very quickly, irrespective of the age difference and had great respect for elders. Surojit immediately bowed down to touch the feet of the Bannerjee couple to obtain their blessings. Despite his upbringing in Delhi, the traditional culture and customs were reflected in his body language. It was very hard to find such a polite and gentle groom in this generation.

Mr Bannerjee said, "I saw your son when he was 10 years old and now, I see a gentleman. Time flies like anything."

Mr Basu replied, "Yes, and I saw your daughter when she was 7 years old. Where is she now? Is she not at home?"

Mr Bannerjee said, "Yes, yes! She is in her room. She was also eagerly waiting for you all."

Having said that, he asked Arunima to call her daughter. Binita came into the room with her mother and then greeted all of them with a smiling face. She bowed down to take their blessings. Mr Basu then introduced her to his son.

Binita greeted him with a smiling face and uttered, "Hi!"

Then they all settled down on the couch...

Chapter 2

When all the elders were busy talking to each other, Binita and Surojit were seated quietly and were lost in silent communication between themselves. Mr Bannerjee noticed that and asked Binita to take Surojit to the rooftop balcony garden.

Binita took him to the balcony where they settled down comfortably.

Binita began the conversation. "Is this your first visit to Kolkata?

Surojit replied, "No, I have come to the city several times during my college projects with my friends."

"So, do you like Kolkata? asked Binita.

"Yes, I do. That's the reason that I agreed to relocate here with my family. The food is good here. The girls are beautiful, too. Besides, Kolkata is the reflection of our culture and traditions."

"Yeah, that's true... But I also heard that when it comes to Delhi, the street food, the shopping corners, the tourist spots, historical monuments and girls are beautiful there, too," said Binita.

Surojit said, "Well, they are beautiful. But you won't get the charm of Bengal anywhere else."

"I see! So, where are you joining?" asked Binita.

"I am joining Softech," said Surojit. "What about you?"

"I am in the final year of my management course," replied Binita.

"Oh really! What's your major?" asked Surojit.

"Human Resources Management and Marketing Management," said Binita.

"Interesting. Dual specialization, huh? Nice! That's great to know," Surojit replied, sounding impressed. "So, what are your plans after completing your final exams?"

"Well, after completing the course, I will be looking for a job in the corporate sector," said Binita.

"Are you planning to look for a job here in Bengal or some other parts of India?" asked Surojit.

"I'll try in Bengal first. If I don't get a good one here, I'll move to other cities," said Binita.

Surojit nodded. Over the course of the conversation, they realized that they liked each other's company.

Mrs Arunima then called both of them for lunch, which was already served on the table. The families took their respective places except Arunima.

Then they all ate with great relish. Mr Basu appreciated the various dishes that Mrs Arunima had prepared. Surojit and Binita sat next to each other.

After lunch, both the fathers went to the rooftop balcony to smoke. There, Mr Basu asked Banerjee where was he planning to get his daughter married.

In reply, Mr Bannerjee said that he had not decided anything yet, as his daughter's wish was to settle down with a job first, become independent, and get married only then.

"Hmm, I see!" said Mr Basu blowing out the smoke. He gazed absently at the sky and asked, "Has she already chosen anyone, as far as your knowledge goes?"

"Well, I don't think so. As parents, we are very close to Binita. If she were interested in someone, she would have informed us."

Basu then said, "Your daughter is very adorable and I wish to bring her to my family as my daughter. What do you say? Do you like my Surojit?"

Banerjee replied, "Yes, of course. Surojit stole my heart, too, with his soft and charming nature. Who wouldn't want him as a son-in-law? I don't have a son and I see a son in Surojit.

I am very delighted with this proposal."

Mr Bannerjee said and continued, "Let her final exams get over and let her start looking for jobs. Until then, both Surojit and Binita can meet occasionally and get to know each other better. She wants to become independent... that's her wish."

Mr Basu agreed, "Yes, that's a wonderful decision of hers. Let her take time. And when she is ready to get married, we can proceed. We are in no hurry."

Binita and Surojit started meeting occasionally thereafter. They were not officially engaged. They wanted to know each other first. And they both decided together to proceed only if they liked each other's company.

After the first meeting, Surojit started developing a soft corner for her. It was love at first sight for him as Binita was very pretty. But he did not express anything to her yet. He would look forward to their meetings and would groom nicely to impress her. He would always buy nice bouquets for her.

Their first meeting after the family lunch was in a coffee shop.

It was Binita's last day of exams. She returned from college after completing it. Her parents asked her how it went. Her father said, "You are done with your formal education. You are going to be an MBA graduate now. You are going to move to the next phase of life. It's time to start a new job and a new life. My darling is growing up."

Binita hugged her father with love and emotion and heaved a great sigh of relief. After lots of hard work, she was finally free from her exam tension.

Then she dressed up for her first meeting with Surojit. It had been three months since their family lunch. Her mother and father were super excited about their daughter's meeting. Her mother helped her select a beautiful dress, but Binita was annoyed.

"Mom! I am not facing any marriage proposal. It is just a casual meeting. Moreover, he already met me once, and there is nothing new about me," she said.

Her dad said, "We know that, darling. But you are officially going on a date today. So, it should be a special one."

"Dad!" Binita protested, stunned.

Chapter 3

At the first meeting, they both were a little bit reserved and formal. Neither of them knew where to start the conversation.

Surojit had reached the venue first and he was browsing on his mobile while waiting.

Binita arrived at the spot and started looking around to find the table where Surojit was seated. When she spotted him, she came towards him and pulled up a chair to sit.

Surojit immediately rose to welcome her, saying, "Hi, how are you?"

"I am good. Thank you," Binita replied with a smile.

"Please be seated," said Surojit."

They were both feeling slightly shy. Eventually, Surojit cleared his throat and asked, "What would you like to have?"

"Well! Nothing, actually," said Binita. "I am full. I had a late lunch at home after I returned from college."

"At least have something light," Surojit persuaded, sliding the menu card toward her.

"Anything is fine," Binita said.

"Okay, then! How about some fritters and coffee?" asked Surojit.

"Yeah, sure," said Binita with a smile.

"So, how was your exam? How were your papers?" asked Surojit.

"They were good," said Binita.

"That's great!" Surojit smiled. "Do you have any vacation plans with your friend now that your exams are over?"

"No, I have a few interviews lined up in the next few weeks, so I would be busy with them," said Binita.

"Oh, that's cool. All the very best. I know you would do great," said Surojit.

"Thanks," said Binita, blushing a bit.

"By the way, have you ever been to Delhi?" Surojit changed the topic.

"Yes, a few times," said Binita.

"Did you like Delhi?"

"No, not much!"

"Why? Is there any particular reason?"

"I don't really know. I felt that the people were too rude, rough and tough. Maybe it's my opinion... but those who live in Delhi never want to go elsewhere. So, I am sure there must be something good about that place," said Binita.

"Well, I can take you to Delhi if you want. Since I was born and brought up there, I have very fond memories of the city. I know many good places and have lots of family friends who still live there. I hope you would like their company as well," said Surojit.

Binita nodded with a smile.

The waiter arrived meanwhile with the fritters and the coffee.

Surojit then asked, "May I ask you a personal question, if you don't mind?"

"Oh, sure. Please go ahead," said Binita.

"So, do you have a boyfriend?"

Binita replied, "No, not yet."

"Such a beautiful girl not having a boyfriend yet! That's strange. I don't believe it," said Surojit.

"Why is it necessary that all beautiful girls should have a

boyfriend?" asked Binita.

"No, no! That's not what I meant. Nowadays, all beautiful girls are engaged or in a relationship. So I thought maybe I would not have any chance with you," Surojit muttered in a soft voice.

"Wha... What?" Binita stuttered, wondering if she had misheard.

"No, nothing," Surojit said with a shy smile, his eyes fixed on her.

Binita suddenly felt shy and lowered her eyes. But eventually working up the courage, she raised her head and asked him, "What about you? Do you have any...?"

"No, I didn't find anyone as beautiful as you," said Surojit, arresting her with his eyes again.

There was silence for a moment.

"So... what kind of person do you want to get married to?" asked Surojit.

"I want someone who would understand me... who would be loving, caring, kind and empathetic. I want someone who would never try to control me... More importantly, we have to be like-minded. His tastes and interests should match mine. We should always have respect for each other. I need someone who would never dominate me," said Binita.

"Haha! Your list appears a bit long," said Surojit with a tricky smile.

Binita did not have a reply for it, and both of them took a sip of coffee from their cups.

Chapter 4

Binita attended a few interviews shortly after. One day, she was in the reception of an office for her interview with the company. She was reading a business magazine while she awaited her turn.

A woman came, calling out her name. "Binita?"

Binita stood up and went inside with her. She finished her interview successfully, re-entered her details at the reception, and went down to where her father was waiting for her in a car. They drove to a mall where Binita and her father coincidentally met Mr Basu and Surojit.

"Hi, Hrishi, nice to see you! So where are you guys heading?" asked Mr Basu.

"We came to get some gifts for my neighbour. It's their marriage anniversary tomorrow," said Mr Bannerjee.

Binita greeted Mr Basu and smiled at Surojit.

Surojit also greeted Mr Bannerjee. "Hello, uncle."

Mr Bannerjee patted Surojit on his back with the words, "How are you, young man?"

"I am doing good, uncle," said Surojit.

Mr Basu immediately said, "Hrishi, it is good that you are here! Why don't you help me with finding something? And let the children have some fun with each other."

Mr Banerjee agreed, and both of them walked away.

Binita tried calling her dad back, but he ignored her as if he didn't hear anything. She was feeling a little uncomfortable at being left alone with Surojit suddenly.

"Is everything alright?" asked Surojit.

"Oh, yes!" said Binita.

They both sat in a corner with shy, smiling faces.

"Well, I forgot to take down your number the other day..." Surojit began.

"You can note it down now," Binita said casually.

Surojit took out his mobile and saved her number.

"Are you nervous?" asked Surojit.

"No, why should I be nervous?" asked Binita.

"Hmm... on seeing me suddenly..." Surojit trailed off.

"No, not at all. It's just that I was not expecting you here," said Binita.

"Yeah, I know," said Surojit. "But are you happy to see me?"

"Yes, I am happy to see you and uncle. It's nice to see him again! My dad is also very pleased to find him," said Binita.

Surojit had been expecting a different answer from Binita. However, he didn't press the point as it was quite personal. And then there was silence for a while. Both of them were short of words and were looking anywhere else but at each other. Then Surojit spoke in a whisper, without even looking at her. "Can I call you and text you sometime?"

"Yeah, sure," said Binita.

Surojit felt very happy from within.

And they both sat quietly for a while when suddenly both their parents returned with shopping bags in their hands. Seeing them, the younger pair stood up with a smile. All of them bade goodbye at once and took their respective paths towards their cars.

Also, Mr Basu reminded Hrishi and Binita, saying, "Don't forget the dinner at our place for Surojit's mother's birthday the day after tomorrow."

Chapter 5

At night, Binita was on the bed when her mobile suddenly beeped. Surojit had sent her a message.

'Hi! This is Surojit.'

Binita was happy to see his message and replied, *'Hi!'*

Surojit's reply came quickly. *'Did I disturb you?'*

'No! Not at all.'

'What were you doing?' asked Surojit.

'Well, I was getting ready to sleep.' Binita replied.

'I was not able to sleep, so I thought of texting you.' Surojit replied, following it up with. *'Can I call you for a minute?'*

'Yes.' replied Binita.

Surojit called Binita immediately.

"Hi, sorry to bother you at this hour! But then, I wanted to ask you something," said Surojit.

"Yes, what's that?" asked Binita.

"Can we meet tomorrow?" Surojit asked.

"Tomorrow? Why? Is there any particular reason? We are anyway meeting the day after tomorrow at your house for lunch," Binita said slowly.

"Yes, I know. But it's very important," said Surojit.

"Okay, but I have an interview tomorrow," Binita hesitated.

"Well, I can pick you up after the interview," Surojit offered.

"Okay. I will text you the time and address," said Binita.

"Bye. Good night. See you tomorrow." Surojit wished and they ended the call.

Chapter 6

Binita finished her interview and got into the lift. She came to the ground floor and saw Surojit waiting for her in the lobby.

"Hi," Binita greeted him.

"Hi, how was your interview?" asked Surojit.

"It was good," replied Binita.

Then they got into the lift together, went down to the basement, and got into the car.

In the car, Binita asked Surojit, "Is everything alright?"

"Yes," said Surojit, and spoke further as he was driving. "Well, actually, I wanted to gift something precious to my mom. But I don't know what it could be. I want to surprise her, and I think you could help me in making the right decision for her."

"Oh, how lovely," said Binita. "Your mother must be so happy to have a lovely and caring son like you. So, what do you want to gift her?"

"Maybe something precious, like a diamond," said Surojit.

"Ok, so how about studs or earrings?" asked Binita.

"Yes, absolutely. I think she would love that because she is quite fond of jewellery," said Surojit.

"Where are we heading now?" asked Binita.

"We are heading to a temple. And from there, we could visit Maxx Mall," replied Surojit.

"Do you visit temples very often?" asked Binita.

"I never visited any temple by myself. I only go if I have to, on family functions or occasions," said Surojit.

"So, what made you want to visit today?" asked Binita.

"Today, for the first time in my life, I felt like visiting the temple and thanking God for something that he gave me," said Surojit.

"Oh, I see," Binita smiled.

They parked the car near the temple and got down to visit the temple. They then worshipped the deities sincerely.

Surojit prayed for the gods' blessings and more power, strength and courage to propose to Binita. He also requested that the gods would make Binita's heart feel for him. He

finished his worshipping with this plea and kept on staring at Binita who was engrossed in prayers.

Then they left the temple and went to a mall. There they made the selection for Surojit's mother. Suddenly, Surojit decided to suggest something else he had wanted to do too.

"Do you have time now? Can we watch a movie?" Surojit asked.

"Now?" Binita responded, looking at her watch.

"Yes."

"Well... I think. It will be too late. Besides, I didn't inform my parents about this and they may be worried if I return late," said Binita.

"You can inform them now," Surojit suggested. "I am sure they won't mind. And I can drop you at home safely after we watch the movie," said Surojit.

Binita agreed. Then they went to the theatre, where they chose a random movie. Binita was busy watching the movie, but Surojit did not miss the chance to keep watching her.

After the Movie, as they walked out of the hall, Surojit asked, "Did you like the movie?"

"Yes. It was a nice one," replied Binita.

From there, they walked to the restaurant which was in the same mall.

The restaurant had a pleasant ambience. It was dimly lit, and there was soft music in the background.

"Hello," the usher at the door greeted them. "How may I help you?"

"We have a booking for two," said Surojit.

"Well, Sir. Could you please confirm your name?" The usher asked. When Surojit gave him the name, he checked the register and asked them to follow him. He took them to a nice corner table, pulled up their seats, and handed menu cards to both of them.

Initially, they were lost in the background music and felt short of words. Both were quiet for a while, lost in thoughts. Binita was on her phone. Surojit stared at her for a minute silently. And then he broke the silence by asking her what she wanted to order. They both selected an item each. The waiter came and took down the order after offering them two glasses of water.

Then Surojit started the conversation, "Binita I wanted to tell you something, if you don't mind."

"Yes, please go ahead."

"I don't know the reason, but I like meeting you and talking

to you over and over again. Nowadays, I cannot even concentrate on anything else. Truly speaking, I see you everywhere. I don't know what this is, because I never experienced anything like that before. I think I am in love," Surojit rushed through his words.

Binita didn't know how to react to the proclamation, so she wordlessly kept her eyes down, feeling slightly nervous. And then Surojit asked again, in a very soft voice, "Do you also feel the same?"

She nodded her head. Then, mainly to ease her nervousness, Surojit said, "Ah! I am sorry. I am making you feel uncomfortable now."

Binita smiled as she said, "No, that's fine."

And then Surojit asked, "If I say that I want to marry you, will you accept?"

Binita was quiet. She had not expected him to come up with such a question at such an early stage of their relationship.

"Binita, please say something. I am getting restless."

And then Binita spoke, "I don't know. It's just been a few days since we met. I would need some more time to make my decision."

"Well, that's perfectly fine!" said Surojit. "I am sure that you also must know that our parents insist that we meet each

other so that we know each other better, right?"

"Yes, I know," said Binita.

"So, can we meet every day from now onwards?" asked Surojit.

"Every day? I don't think that would be good, because I don't want to put you in more trouble. I think we should give each other some more time and space. This could be an infatuation," said Binita.

With a chuckle, Surojit asked, "So, how long do you want to take?"

"Well, I don't know. I would wait for my heart to respond naturally," said Binita.

"Do you not like me?" asked Surojit.

"Of course, I like you. You are a family friend and you are a nice person. But then, liking someone as a person and liking someone as a partner for the rest of your life is different. And when it comes to the decision of our lifetime... I think, instead of being in a hurry, we can take more time to be sure about our feelings," said Binita.

"Yeah, you are right," Surojit agreed. The food had arrived by then. Their waiter served the food and left quietly. Surojit and Binita took bites of their food.

Chapter 7

Binita was sitting at her study table with a reading lamp glowing softly.

She turned the book page by page, but she could not concentrate. His words continually flashed in her mind, so she could not focus. Giving up, she closed the book and sat beside the window. She felt restless.

Then she tried to get into the bed and closed her eyes, but she didn't get sleep. She took her mobile to check if there were any messages from Surojit.

But there was none.

So she typed a few words. *'Hi, hope all is well.'*

But she hesitated before sending, backspaced the message, lay down on her side, and tried to sleep holding a pillow tight over her heart.

She dreamt of Surojit and herself in a beautiful garden staring at each other.

*****

The day of the party arrived and the Banerjees were planning to visit Surojit's house. It was a 'limited invitees' party. Only 4-5 families were invited.

Surojit's father was busy welcoming the guests. Mrs Basu was also busy with guests and arrangements, and Surojit was eagerly waiting for Mr Bannerjee's family to arrive. He kept frequently checking the time on his watch.

Mrs Basu called Surojit and asked him to check if the musicians were ready to start with the live music for the evening. Right then, Mr Basu's excited voice proclaimed, "Welcome, welcome! Here is the chief guest of the evening."

He was greeting Mr Bannerjee's family and welcomed Mr Bannerjee with a hug. Surojit was mesmerized by Binita's dress and makeup. He was dumbstruck by her beauty and elegance.

Mr Basu introduced the family to his other friends and families. Strangely, Surojit was absent from the scene for a few minutes. Binita unconsciously looked for him.

Surojit's heart had started beating erratically the moment he saw her from a distance. But recovering from that, slowly he came near Binita. He greeted her with a smile and expressed all the happiness in his heart.

The live band started playing the music in the background. The attendees of the party looked very well-dressed and were in a party mood.

Surojit stood beside Binita and silently whispered in her ear, "You are looking fabulous. I am not able to take away my eyes from you."

With a soft smile, Binita replied, "Thank you!"

While they were talking, the guests approached the table where a big birthday cake was placed. Mr Basu, Mrs Basu, and Surojit were close to each other. Mrs Basu blew out the candle and cut the cake. Everyone sang the birthday song. The first piece of cake went into Mr Basu's mouth, and he took a little bite. The rest of the piece was shared amongst Mrs Basu and then to their son, Surojit.

The live band then played a very romantic dance number and all the couples there took positions with their partners for the dance.

Some of the young boys and girls were clapping, cheering their parents dancing in tune to the music. Surojit approached Binita and offered his hand, requesting a dance with her.

Binita hesitated. "Thank you, but I can't dance."

Surojit said, "No worries, I will help you dance. Come on!"

Binita nodded her head with a shy smile. Surojit's encouraging hand was still extended towards her and he had bent towards her with a smile. Binita could not turn down his request any longer and joined him on the dance floor.

He held her hands for the first time and gently clasped her waist. Binita's face turned blue with the suppressed emotions, her hands turned cold and her smile disappeared from her face at once. She was nervous. They danced together slowly with a romantic melodious tune. She could not look at him even once, but Surojit kept staring at her with eyes full of love. He did not avert his eyes even for a second.

When the music paused, everyone stopped dancing and there was a huge round of applause. At once, Binita released her hand from Surojit's. And, without turning back, she returned to the couch to talk with other guests. She had also brought a glass of juice in her hand. She couldn't look at Surojit anymore. She had started forming a soft corner for him. She was getting emotional.

After a while, dinner was served. All the families had a great evening and left one by one. Binita's family was the last to leave the house.

Mrs Basu thanked Mr Bannerjee and his family for attending the party and making her day memorable.

Binita bade goodbye to all and Surojit thanked her for coming to the party and for dancing with him.

Blushing, Binita replied, "It was my pleasure."

Chapter 8

For the next couple of days, there was no call or text from Surojit. Binita was expecting a call or text from him and was wondering why he did not contact her. She was getting restless.

She kept looking at the clocks and calendars throughout the day, and her mobile screen every few minutes to check if there was any text from him.

On the 4th day, her phone suddenly rang. She had been preparing for an interview that was slated for the next day, so her phone was put on charge on the other side of the room.

The moment she heard the ringtone, she beamed with joy, thinking that it was a call from Surojit. She ran to check her phone but her happiness disappeared when she saw that the call was from an unknown number. She picked up the phone and said, "Hello!"

The voice on the other side said, "Hi, Binita! This is Christine. I am calling from Eco-Business Tech. How are you doing today?"

"I am doing well. Thank you."

"I called to discuss further options based on the interview you had with us a week ago. We would like to move to the next level and would like to schedule another round of interviews with you. Are you available the day after tomorrow at 11 AM?"

"Yes, I am."

"Great. Thank you for letting us know. I will send you a calendar invite. See you at the office, then. Have a good day. Bye."

Binita replied, "Wishing you a good day, too. Thank you. Bye."

Despite the good news about being selected for the next round of interviews, she was upset from within. When she thought about it, she realized that she missed Surojit badly. She took her phone and looked at his profile picture.

Chapter 9

Surojit was at work. He tried to keep himself busy and calm. He had just spoken to his boss about a project and they finished a meeting. He had flown to Delhi for work with his teammates.

Binita returned from her college. When she arrived home, she saw Surojit's family car parked at their door. She hurriedly got out of her car and entered her house with a smile, her heart beating in happiness, assuming that Surojit might have visited. She held her breath and stepped into the house slowly and nervously.

As she proceeded, she could hear the voice of Surojit's parents from the entrance.

They were having tea and talking about their college days.

Mr Basu said, "Do you still remember Anupam? The short and intelligent guy."

"Yes, Anupam! Where is he nowadays?" asked Mr Basu.

"He is in Chennai, taking care of his in-laws' family business. I met him in Delhi 3 years ago. He has changed a lot. He took an early retirement from his high-paying job and decided to

start an organic farm in Chennai in collaboration with his father-in-law. He is not the reserved, serious guy anymore, after all these years. His children are well settled. His daughter is married to an industrialist from Punjab and lives in Delhi, and his son is in Los Angeles. It felt good to talk to him. He is associated with an NGO. I heard that he is also helping the needy through his organization."

"That's nice to know. I still remember our last football match with Anupam and his team, and the fight that took place with our opponent team's goalkeeper. Those days, we all were so serious about the fight. But now when we look back, it only brings smiles to my face as I realise that it was just a silly affair!"

Their conversation went on like that. Binita walked forward, and as soon as she stepped into the drawing, room she could see them.

"Here comes my daughter," said Mr Bannerjee.

Binita smiled and greeted the visitors. She then enquired if Surojit had not come.

Mr Basu replied, "He is in Delhi for some work."

"When did he travel?" Binita asked, astonished.

"He left this morning," Mrs Basu informed her. "Why, did he not inform you?"

"No," Binita said, shaking her head.

"Oh! He might have missed informing you... he left in a hurry," said Mrs. Basu.

"How many days will he be on this trip?" Binita asked slowly.

Mr Basu replied, "He said he would be travelling for a week, but it actually depends on his project. It might take longer than that. Apparently, they need to set up a new team in the Delhi office."

"Oh, I see," Binita nodded.

Then Mr and Mrs Basu got ready to leave. And just before they started, they said, "Let us have frequent evening chats like this. The next tea meeting is at our place."

The Banerjees agreed and waved off the other couple. But as she watched them go, Binita was disappointed that she had neither seen nor heard from Surojit.

For the next few days, she kept herself engaged in reading books before bedtime, going for morning walks, visiting children from the nearby orphanage and, sometimes, sitting alone in a park, thinking about Surojit.

She remembered all her meetings with him, his smile, his words, his greetings, his appreciation...

A week passed by and there was no message or call from

him, nor any news about his return. Every time she would check her mobile but would not find any text or call from him. Sometimes she would listen to her dad's phone call with Basu Uncle from behind the door, to find out if there was any news about Surojit.

Time flew by, and it was now fifteen days since she had last heard of – or from – Surojit. On the 16ᵗʰ Day, her father dropped her at the interview venue.

"Bye, dear. And all the best!" He smiled at her before leaving.

She entered the office, registered at the reception, and waited for her turn. She was called inside after a while. The interviewer asked a few questions, and Binita answered all of them. She then took his leave with a smile.

When she came out of the lift, her phone suddenly rang. It was a call from Surojit.

Her heart started beating hard merely on seeing his name displayed on the screen after fifteen long days. She held the phone close to her heart, closed her eyes, and took a deep breath before attending the call. She looked for a silent corner to talk freely.

Her hand was trembling as she finally accepted the call and muttered, "Hello."

"Hi, how are you?" asked Surojit.

"I am good! What about you?" Binita asked with a smile.

"I am doing good too. Are you outside?"

"Yes, I am!"

"Where are you?" Surojit asked directly.

"I am in St. Martha Street. Just finished with an interview," Binita informed him.

"Oh, okay. Do you have any other plans for the evening?" he asked.

"No, I don't have any particular plans," said Binita.

"Well, then... Can we meet today at 5 PM?"

"Yes, sure," Binita agreed with a smile.

"Okay, then. Could you come to St. Martha Street again and wait in front of the cathedral there? I will pick you up from there..." Surojit suggested.

"Sure," said Binita.

"See you then. Bye. Take care," said Surojit.

Binita said likewise and cut the call with a huge smile. Her joy knew no bounds. She was excited to meet him.

Getting out of the office quickly, she reached home, kept her bag and keys on the surface of the shoe cabinet, and called her dad. He was in the kitchen. She ran to him and, out of joy, hugged him tight and danced around him.

Her dad was surprised to see her overwhelmed face and asked her what the matter was. "You seem to be very happy today!" He observed.

"Yes, Dad. I am elated!" Binita agreed, laughing. "What are you preparing now?"

"Well, I am trying to bake your mom's favourite fruit cake. She would be delighted to see this when she returns home from work. We can have this cake together with tea in the evening," Mr Banerjee smiled.

He poured the batter from the mixing cup onto a tray and spoke while he worked. "All these years, your mom took care of us. She took care of all our needs, big and small, even after working long days and taking care of the house. She always tried to serve me good food whenever I returned from a tiring day. Now, it's my turn to look after her. Isn't it?"

While he was talking, he had taken some fresh fruits from the big fruit bowl and placed them on the chopping board.

Binita wrapped her arms around her father's shoulder and kissed him on the cheek as she said, "Yes, Dad! You are a caring father and a very caring husband." Then she added, "Let me get freshened up and help you in cutting the fruits."

She left the room, smiling to hear her father singing as he was cutting the fruits. She returned to the kitchen in a short while and took another knife to help her father. She settled on a chair and started cutting some more fruits.

Her father reminded her, "You did not yet share the reason for your happiness with me. What made you so particularly happy today?"

She felt shy to tell him the truth. Instead, she told her father, "My interview went well today and I am looking forward to the next steps."

"Oh, really!" Mr Banerjee exclaimed. "By the way, you attended many other interviews in the last few weeks, and I didn't hear anything about them from you!"

"Well, I got through many of them. But then, they were not exactly the kind of jobs that I was looking for. In some places, the pay was good but the profile was not up to the mark, whereas in some other places, the profile was okay, but the pay was very low. There were also a few cases where they didn't have any openings here in the city and instead wanted me to move to another city. And I don't want to be away from you and Mom," said Binita feeling emotional.

"Hmm, is your worry about being away from us or Surojit?" Mr Banerjee asked with a tricky smile.

"No, Dad. Why him?" Binita deflected with a smile.

"By the way, when are you guys meeting again?" He asked, seemingly casually.

"Oh, I forgot to inform you. He suddenly called me today after the interview, and asked me to meet him at 5 PM," said Binita. "I don't know when he returned from Delhi, she added as an afterthought.

Mr Banerjee said, "Oh, yes! Even I forgot to mention to you that Mr Basu informed me at around 7 PM last night that he was going to pick up his son from the airport at 11.30 PM. It is good that Surojit has already called you today. So, how far have you guys progressed in the relationship?" Mr Banerjee asked, adding the fruits as garnishing to the baking tray.

Astonished, Binita asked, "Relationship? What, Dad? Why should we be in such a hurry? I haven't gotten a job yet. And I definitely haven't thought of anything of that sort," said Binita.

He finished garnishing and placed the tray on the oven, saying, "That's okay, darling. But it's not good to make someone suffer in the pain of love."

He turned around, took up his baking gloves and placed them on the slab. Then, again, he spoke while looking into her eyes. "If you haven't thought of it already, then you should start thinking about that without any further delay."

"What do you mean, dad? I didn't get you. Who is suffering?" asked Binita, still feeling confused and astonished.

"I can very clearly see the love in his eyes for you. And you know one thing? However strong boys seem to be when it comes to love, they are actually very weak and sensitive. The only difference is that they always don't show them clearly, and you can never measure their feelings from their body language. What you see in Surojit is special. His depth of love for you is way beyond usual, and you cannot easily see it at first," said Mr Banerjee.

Chuckling, Binita asked, "How do you know so much, Dad?"

"Because that's how I was, and I am. And I too loved your mother the way he loves you. That's why I know what's going on with him. I can measure his feelings and could relate to him. In your journey of life, you will meet many people. But you won't find true love everywhere. It is rare to find. And if you find one, you should never let it go. Besides, I can read your face and mind too, my sweet little girl! I knew that you missed him all these days during his absence from the city. Am I right?" He smiled.

Feeling emotional and having tears in her eyes, Binita said, "Oh, Dad! I love you."

Mr Banerjee also held her tight and patted her on her back. That was the first ever time in her memory that Binita took time to dress up for a meeting because meeting with Surojit before had been pleasant and normal. But after the conversation today, it looked and felt quite significant. It was a call from the heart.

Chapter 10

Binita was in a beautiful dress, waiting for Surojit near the cathedral.

In a few minutes, Surojit pulled the car towards her and picked her up. He remained in the driver's seat and did not get down to greet her, as if he was in a hurry.

"So, where do you want to go? Do you know any beautiful place that won't be crowded much?" asked Surojit.

"The choice is yours," said Binita with a smile.

"Ok, Your Highness!" Surojit said, grinning.

He drove his car out of the city and towards a countryside farmland. He parked his car by the road and both of them walked around in the lush pastures which also had farm animals. They sat on a bench there, a respectable space between them. They both were quiet for a while, just enjoying the beautiful scenery.

Binita broke the silence. "I didn't hear from you for the last two weeks, so I was wondering if you were doing alright." She paused, and then added, "I was expecting your call. You didn't even inform me before you had to go to Delhi."

"I was doing fine. I thought since I was not that important to you, it was not necessary to inform you of such a small official tour. Also, in our last meeting, you said that we both need to give each other some time and space. So I thought of not bothering you for a while," said Surojit.

Binita nodded, agreeing to that, not knowing what to reply further.

But Surojit got up from the bench, walked a few steps forward, turned his back towards Binita and muttered, "I don't know about you, but I tried to stay away from you during the trip without any form of contact. But these 15 days looked like 15 years to me. I couldn't stop thinking about you, Binita. I couldn't stop dreaming about you. I am sorry. I couldn't stop loving you, either. And I don't know whether you have feelings for me or not... but I know that I am deeply in love with you."

His emotional words made it clear that Surojit's heart was full of love for her.

And then, he took a deep breath. Turning his head slightly in her direction, he asked, "Did your heart speak to you? Waiting for something is so painful, Binita. And you won't know the pain of it until you experience that personally."

"Yes, I know. And yes, my heart did speak to me this time. I missed you and I am sorry to have hurt you this way."

Surojit couldn't believe his ears. With a smile, he turned around and asked, "What? Did you say you missed me? Really? No, no, it can't be... Say that again!"

"Yes, I said I missed you," Binita agreed, and then added, "Sometimes, distance brings people closer to each other."

Binita looked at Surojit with a smile. He came closer to her, hesitated just a minute, and took out a beautifully packaged rose from his pocket. Then he stretched his arm towards her while he knelt on one knee, and said, "I love you, Binita."

Binita stood up from the bench and accepted it with a smile.

"By the way, how did you know that I would agree to meet today and you would get a chance to give me a rose stick? It looks like you came prepared," Binita teased.

"I always carried a rose stick inside my shirt but never got a chance to offer it to you. I was always waiting for this day," said Surojit.

He stood back up and continued, "This is not just a red rose, but my heart. I am leaving my heart with you from today onwards. Keep it safe."

Binita nodded with a smile again, feeling shy.

"So, can I call you daily hereafter?" asked Surojit.

"Yes," Binita replied.

Surojit exclaimed in joy, pumping his fists as he hopped and jumped around exuberantly. It looked like he had gone mad on hearing her acceptance.

Binita laughed loudly. Surojit was happy to see her laughing so loudly, expressing her feelings so openly. It was the first time he had seen it! They both were very happy and laughed with the carefree innocence of young love.

Chapter 11

Binita got a call on her mobile. The woman on the other end spoke with a crisp voice.

"Hi, this is Christine again. How are you doing?"

"I am doing good. Thank you for asking. How are you doing today?"

"I am doing good, too. And I have some good news for you. You have been shortlisted for our company, and we are offering you the position. I will send you an email right away with the details. Go through that and respond to us as soon as possible. If you have any questions, you can reach out to me at any time."

"Thank you very much. I will surely check and confirm about it at the earliest. Thank you once again, and have a good day," said Binita.

"You too, bye!" said Christine.

Binita ran to her parents and shared the good news. She hugged them both tightly and jumped in happiness. Her father then said, "Go and share the news with your life partner now!"

Binita nodded, "Yes, Papa!"

Her mother also smiled with happiness and leaned her head on her father's shoulder.

*****

Binita and Surojit were in a restaurant.

"So, what's next?" asked Surojit.

Binita merely smiled, not saying a word.

"When is your date of joining?" Surojit prompted.

"Next Monday," Binita informed him.

"Congrats!" Surojit said, smiling at her.

"Does that mean that next month we are getting married?" asked Surojit.

"Noooooo!" Binita said, looking stunned. "Let me join first. Besides, we need more time for wedding preparation. Next month is too early!"

"How much longer will you make me wait, Binita? I cannot wait anymore. I am dying. I cannot stop myself from holding you close to my heart. Shall I talk to my parents regarding this? So we could at least begin the proceedings?" Surojit demanded, the passion clear in his eyes.

She nodded and said, "Yes, you can!"

The food arrived by then. Binita took the first bite while Surojit stared at her silently. She lifted her chin unconsciously and caught him staring.

Now feeling conscious, she asked, "What's wrong?"

Surojit shook his head. "Nothing. I have every right to stare at my would-be wife from today onwards!"

Binita felt shy and ducked her head, averting her eyes with a blush. He continued to stare at her, unabashedly.

After a while, she uttered without lifting her face, "Will you please stop staring at me?"

He shook his head again, a hint of playfulness not managing to alter the seriousness of his tone. "I want to look into your eyes like this day and night!"

When she did not reply, he continued. "I cannot make you understand just how much you mean to me, Binita. I don't know how am I going to spend this night. The moment I drop you at home, my countdown to meeting you the next day starts. My colleagues say that I am meandering aimlessly in the office these days. The reality is that I just wait to see you again the next day. I am totally in love with you. I am completely lost with how overwhelming it is. If you have any medicine for this, then please help me with that!"

Binita looked up at him again from the opposite end of the table. Then she whispered, "I love you."

"Say that again," said Surojit.

"I love you," Binita repeated more firmly.

Hearing that, Surojit became still like a statue, held his chest with both his palms, and pretended to fall from his chair. Binita laughed at his antics, got up, and walked out of the restaurant. Surojit followed her to the car, ruffling his hair up with a goofy grin. He got into the driving seat, fastened his seat belt, and drove out of the place.

After that, their meetings continued with more intensity. They met every day and in the process got to know each other much better. The venue for their meetings was never the same twice in a row. They roamed happily throughout the city, enjoying their days in cafes, restaurants, shopping malls, parks, book stalls, libraries, and even in temples and churches. They even met at the birthday party of one of his colleagues.

Binita and Surojit realized how much they had in common when they both loved the long drives away from the hustle or when they visited orphanages and old age homes to spend some quality time with the inmates of those places. Their love grew in strength and solidified as they bonded over these meetings.

Chapter 12

Binita and Surojit's relationship had progressed wonderfully and become official.

Both the Basu and Banerjee families met in a temple to discuss with a priest and decide on a date for the wedding. Binita looked fabulous on that day in traditional attire.

The Pandit ji chose an auspicious date a month away, and everything got finalized. After fixing the date, the elders returned home, leaving both of them alone.

Binita and Surojit visited a lake park after they left the temple, and decided to spend a while there. They sat on a park bench.

Surojit turned to her and asked, "Now that our wedding is finalized, may I have your permission to hold your hands, please?!"

That was the first day that Binita allowed him to hold her hands, for she had always been reserved with her values.

Binita smiled wordlessly and indicated her acceptance with her eyes. Surojit slowly sat closer to her on the bench and then held her hands tight. Binita felt pleasant tingles at the touch. Then, on an unspoken agreement, they rose and walked together towards the lake, their joined hands swinging between them. They enjoyed the nice evening with the view of the sun setting.

*****

The Day of the Engagement

The friends, relatives and guests of both the families were in their best party attire. The house was decorated with a specially chosen theme and a music band was arranged to both entertain and provide a mellow background for the event.

The young couple was the centre of attraction. Binita and Surojit sat opposite each other for the ring ceremony, which was done with much pomp. After the ring exchange, a big round of applause drowned any other sounds in the hall. The party started then, full of songs, couple-dance numbers, and catered food.

Once the ceremony ended, Surojit's and Binita's families went to their family deity's temple to seek blessings. After the prayer, the new couple stood together in silence in front of God. Binita looked nervous.

Noticing her discomfort, Surojit asked, "What's the matter? Why are you looking very tense?"

Binita shook her head, "I don't know why, but some rather unwelcome thoughts overpowered my mind, and I am feeling very nervous."

Surprised, Surojit asked, "What's the matter? You can share anything with me. Maybe I would be able to resolve your worry!"

"I am going to step into a new life with a new family and a new life partner. From my childhood, I was in the shade of my parents' love and was always pampered like a kid. But I don't know how my new life would be. I would no longer share the same house with my parents. I cannot see them every day. I would not be able to eat my mom's special dishes any more. My dad would feel lonely and alone during my mom's absence during the day. And on top of that, I would have more responsibilities as a wife and daughter-in-law.

"There may also be some other expectations of me, which I am not aware of now. I am not sure if I would be able to manage everything and earn a good name for myself and my parents too! Right now, everything looks beautiful and rosy. But a marriage is not an easy task. Would I be able to take care of you all the time? Would I be able to take care of your family's needs as required? There is so much of worry!" said Binita.

Smiling softly at her candid words, Surojit said, "I understand, Binita. I can totally understand your worry. I realise it would take time for you to settle down in a new life with new people. But I assure you that, from my end, there

won't be any complaints. I will try my best to give you company and take care of you and your needs always. I promise you that I will never let you down. I will give you so much love that you won't have any time to regret or feel sad for anybody or anything that you left behind. Every single day with me would be filled with happiness.

"Besides, if you want, I can drop you at your parents' home every day on your way back home from the office until you are able to settle down comfortably in our house. And you wouldn't be a daughter-in-law to my parents. They already consider you as their daughter and you would be equally pampered in our house like you were in yours. There won't be any expectations from you like the old, traditional ones with daughters-in-law. So, you have nothing to fear about. Everything will be alright with time. And we are in a temple now, a house of God. God never makes his children unhappy. Leave everything in His hands, and let Him decide on your behalf. The rest will fall in place automatically," Surojit said comfortingly.

Feeling emotional at his understanding and love, Binita said, "Thank you!"

Chapter 13

The Wedding Day

Binita was dressing up in her wedding attire in her room. One of her friends helped her set the dress right.

There was a flurry of activity as Binita was then called to the wedding hall for rituals and ceremonies in the presence of the groom and their family, friends and relatives.

The wedding was conducted grandly and was full of frolic, dance, music, and great food. It was the talk of the town.

The couple had taken wedding leaves for two weeks and had enough time to spend well with both the families and also on their baby steps for their life journey together.

The day they had to return to their offices again, Binita and Surojit woke up quite late in the morning. Then they freshened up, dressed, and went to the breakfast table, where Binita found that her in-laws were waiting for them on the table with the breakfast already served.

Binita said, "Sorry, Mom. I woke up late, so couldn't help you in preparation!"

Mrs Basu replied with a smile, "That's alright, darling. You are new to the house. Take some time to settle down, and make yourself at home. And then you can start helping us around the house. There is no hurry. I know it will take time for you to adjust. Moreover, you are not used to the new routine yet. Take your own time. I am like your mother. So don't hesitate and feel free to open up with me like you would do with your mother!"

"Thank you," replied Binita.

They finished their breakfast together and then the newly married couple started together for work after saying their goodbyes to their parents. They got into the car and Surojit drove out of the gate.

Mr and Mrs Basu seemed to be very happy and they talked amongst themselves while they were standing at the door.

"We are very lucky to find her for our beloved son. She is very sweet and caring, isn't she?" Mrs Basu commented.

"Yes, indeed! And now, we don't have to worry about Surojit anymore. He has found the love of his life. And I know my son would never let her down. He will keep her happy," said Mr Basu.

And then, he turned around and wrapped his hands around his wife's shoulder. In a very romantic mood, he asked her, "Did I give you all the happiness? Do you still remember our newly married days?"

"Yes, I do. How can I forget those happy days? And yes, I was also lucky to have you in my life. Since the very first day, you always tried to keep me happy and never gave me any chance to complain. I hope our son will also succeed in his duties likewise."

Chapter 14

Surojit gave Binita a call during office hours.

"What are you doing, my love? I do not feel like working at all. I see you everywhere. I am not able to concentrate on anything else. You have put some kind of magic spell on me, my dear wife. What about you? How are you dealing with work?"

Binita did not pause working, and smiled as she replied, "I am also not feeling like working. But we have to do it. So, I am trying to concentrate."

"Okay, what shall I get for you after work?" asked Surojit.

"Nothing. Now, you are all mine. And we are living together. So what else do I need?"

"But I need something else from you," said Surojit.

Astonished, Binita asked, "Whaaaat? What do you want?"

"You know what I mean. Guess what it is? Well, only you can give it to me."

"Oh! Don't talk rubbish. Go and do your work at your office,

my Prince. I am keeping the phone down now."

She grinned, feeling her heart burst with love at their antics.

That evening, Surojit went to a flower shop and got a bouquet of red roses. Then he drove to Binita's office and picked her up. In the car, he handed the bouquet to her.

Binita asked, "What's this for?"

Surojit replied, "No particular reason. Or rather, one reason. For being my wife. I wanted to say thank you to you for coming into my life."

Binita smiled and replied, "Thank you, my darling husband."

Then they drove back home, chatting happily.

*****

Surojit's parents were seated on the couch when they called the younger couple into the drawing room.

When Surojit and Binita arrived and settled down, Mr Basu handed an envelope to Surojit.

"What is it, dad?" Surojit asked him.

"Just open and see," replied Mr Basu.

Surojit opened the envelope and found travel tickets and hotel booking confirmation.

"Dad, what is all this now?" Surojit muttered, handing the envelope to Binita.

"It is high time you went for your honeymoon, my son. So don't waste your time. Things should be done at the right time. Otherwise, the charm and excitement get lost, you know," Mr Basu smiled.

Both Binita and Surojit thanked them shyly.

*****

They both flew to their honeymoon destination with much anticipation.

The famous tourist spot had everything they wanted to see. They went to beaches, took rides in the amusement park there, did some shopping, and tried all the sumptuous dishes in the local cuisines. On many evenings, they walked by the beach, sat together for hours watching the waves, and spent some quality time with each other.

*****

The happy couple returned from their vacation, feeling refreshed. But after having had restaurant food for a long while, they ate the homemade food with great relish.

"Mom, I feel so good after eating the homemade food made by your hand after so long. I missed it," Surojit praised his mother.

Binita added, "Yes, mom. We were tired of eating restaurant food every day. The magic you have in your hands is not found anywhere else in this world!"

*****

The couple had gone on a shopping spree during their honeymoon. So when both Binita and Surojit's parents were together in the drawing room, they decided to present the gifts they had bought. Binita unpacked and handed over the gifts to everyone, and it was obvious that she had put a lot of thought into it based on what each person needed and liked.

*****

The next Monday, they resumed their regular work at their offices.

Their married life was full of love and happiness together. Every day, Surojit would call Binita during a break from work to check on what she was doing. And every evening, he would gift her a bouquet.

Throughout the days, they spent a lot of time together. Their activities always included the other, and neither of them wanted to do anything alone. Be it watching movies, cooking, cleaning, shopping, taking a walk, eating, driving to work or

any such thing, they would always do it together. It was a special kind of love to go to sleep in each other's arms and wake up like that too.

Surojit never allowed her to clean the vessels or cook any dishes while his parents were away. He would snatch every bit of hard work away from her to keep her hands soft and supple. He would occasionally take her to the parlour for a makeover. He would buy her fashionable dresses to make her look more beautiful and stylish, like a princess.

Binita would also do the same thing for Surojit and spoil him with her care and affection.

They enjoyed even the domestic acts together; they would visit parks and feed birds together, they also planted saplings and indulged in gardening, fishing, and other recreational activities. They visited every place together, be it churches or temples.

Their married life was full of love and excitement, and they were a model couple.

Time flew, and on their third wedding anniversary, Surojit and Binita were in a restaurant with 2 bunches of bouquets beside them. They blew a candle and cut a cake, and then fed it to each other, after which they exchanged gifts.

Surojit gifted her a diamond necklace and Binita gifted him a watch.

"It has been such a nice and memorable journey of three years with each other," said Binita.

"Every day, I just pray to God to keep both of us healthy, safe and sound in every walk of life, and keep us together like this with His blessings. I just want you to be happy, my love. And I want this bond of friendship and love to grow stronger in the days to come," said Surojit.

Binita held his hands and said fervently, "May God always bless us and keep us in His shade. I will always love you, dear."

Then, holding her eyes, Surojit said, "Let us both promise on our special day that we will always be together, whatever comes our way. We should also promise each other that if anything happens to one of us, then the other will stay healthy to take care of our parents and our child who is yet to see the world."

"I promise you, my dear," said Binita.

Then, Surojit held out his hand and helped Binita step out off the table as she was pregnant and heavy.

"Step out slowly, and be careful. We have our next appointment with the Doctor tomorrow," he said softly.

"Yes, I remember," Binita smiled, thankful for his help and love.

Chapter 15

Binita was in the hospital bed with a happy face.

Around her bed stood Surojit and both their parents. Mr Banerjee held the baby girl with excitement and said, "She looks exactly like Binita did when she was born..."

He then transferred the baby gently from his lap to Mr Basu's lap.

Everyone was excited to welcome the new member of their family, and Surojit and Binita were beyond elated.

*****

Binita and Surojit returned home in a car that was well decorated and had a sticker that read: Baby on board.

A new journey with their daughter began from there. Surojit held the newborn baby in his arms as they entered the house. The little girl was their pride and joy and she made the household happy with every passing day.

The grandparents took care of the baby the whole day when Surojit and Binita had to work. In the evening, after they returned, the parents took turns taking care of the baby

including the playing, feeding, cleaning, wiping, and diaper changing routines.

They also took equal responsibility in everything including tucking the baby in for sleep.

At work, they both remained very busy and worked with full concentration. Even though years had gone by, Surojit never forgot to get the flowers for his wife as he used to do before the birth of his daughter. And then, during office hours, he often called and checked on her at regular intervals. It was nearly 4 years since the day they got married, but their bond and relationship were never compromised.

They always lived and acted like a newly married couple who just happened to have some additional responsibilities on their shoulder. They were the dutiful children to their parents, doting parents to their daughter, and a happy couple at home. They also did well in their jobs and were accordingly promoted annually. They attended regular meetings, took responsibility for new projects, got promotions and went for family picnics with the baby on weekends.

It seemed that time flew, for their newborn daughter, Titli, had now grown to be eight years old. Surojit and Binita were the best parents she could have, and they showered all their love on her.

Parenting brought more happiness, responsibilities and liveliness to their lives. They would sit for lessons with their kid, ensuring that she always had someone to help her with her studies. Sometimes, they dropped her school before leaving for their respective offices and sometimes she boarded the school bus.

Firmly believing that a wholesome and happy childhood was essential for their child, Surojit and Binita ensured that they took their child to movies she enjoyed, and libraries where she could develop her reading habits. They got her new books, too.

Their evenings and holidays were times of fun. Surojit would often don a chef's hat and amaze everyone with his cooking skills. They even had fun cooking pizza at home. But sometimes, Surojit could burn a simple thing as an omelette or a flatbread and they would laugh about it happily.

They had game nights and regularly played games as a family of grandparents, parents, and a young child. They lived a happy, meaningful life that they cherished.

Everything was going so well.

*****

It was her 8th birthday, and Titli cut a birthday cake, amidst the sounds of birthday songs. She played with her friends. Gifts were stacked on the tables, and the guests were treated to a variety of pizzas, pasta dishes, salads, fruits, and a multicuisine experience.

Titli was a big girl now and was responsible enough to take care of her parents and grandparents.

In her growing years, Titli was also busy with extra-curricular activities, and she attended many classes like music class, dance class, and painting classes after her school hours.

Part One ends;

Part Two begins now!

Chapter 16

Binita was on a call with her mother.

"Mom, all these days, you had been taking good care of Titli. But you are also ageing. I feel like we are not able to give quality time to Titli as before due to our increasingly busy schedule. Frankly, I am not able to balance work and personal life. I think I should take a break from work to take better care of Titli during these growing years.

"My responsibilities at work are increasing every day, and it will only get more intense in the near future as the company is doing more business and opening up new projects one after the other. And, with all of these happening, it is impossible to focus more at home and find that balance.

"Somewhere, I have to prioritise what matters the most and compromise in my career so I could bring up Titli with more care and focus. She is also growing bigger and the demands in her education will also keep increasing. It is important to focus on that development and prepare her for the rest of her life. After a few years, work might mellow down, and I might have more time for family. But Titli won't have any time for us anymore at that point. She would get busy with her studies and school projects. Let me see what can be done. I will discuss with the management today and see if I get some flexibility and can bring some work home."

Right as she was saying this, Binita suddenly felt hazy and held her chest for a few seconds as she experienced a sudden, peculiar pain there. She had never experienced such pain before.

Noticing the silence, Mrs. Banerjee asked her, "What happened? Is everything all right?"

Binita replied, "Nothing. I experienced an abnormal pain in my chest suddenly. But it disappeared now. I am doing alright. Thanks for asking, Mom."

*****

A few nights later, while both Binita and Surojit were asleep, she woke up in the middle of the night with a prickling pain in her chest. The pain reduced within a few minutes and she went back to sleep without giving it much importance.

Over the next few days, she experienced similar pains occasionally, but every time, it subsided within a few seconds. So, she always ignored it and did not give much importance to it. She also developed a kind of cyst on her breast that was filled with puss. It leaked a fluid when squeezed but did not pain.

On her way back from work one evening, she went to a doctor and got some homoeopathic medicine and ointment for temporary pain relief. After applying it for a few days in the affected area, she was fully cured and there were no further problems at all. Sometimes, when she experienced pain, she handled the situation with one or two doses of

painkillers.

Following through with her thoughts about focusing more on the home front, she applied for 1 year of sabbatical leave to spend more time with her daughter and family. She had no other options. It had been a necessary choice and her own decision, but she was also upset from within. Initially, she decided to continue her leave for a year. And then, depending on the situation, she thought of extending.

Surojit understood her feelings and consoled her. "Don't worry. I am with you. You can start a business from home if you want. That way, you would be able to give time to our daughter while you also do justice to your ideas and have mental satisfaction. I know it was your choice. But at the same time, this is a tough decision to digest for a career-oriented and ambitious woman like you. But don't think much about it. I will always be there beside you, no matter what."

"Thank you, Surojit. That's what I expected from you. I know it will take some time, but I think giving her my time is going to be more important. And with this, I would get the most precious moments of my life," said Binita.

Surojit then asked, "So when is your last day?"

"Next week," replied Binita.

"So don't forget to go for your annual health checkup meanwhile. Shall I book an appointment for you?"

"Yes, please do," replied Binita.

*****

Binita was at the hospital, sitting with a doctor who held the reports of her annual health checkup. The doctor inspected her report and looked a little tense.

She asked Binita, "When was your last checkup?"

Binita replied, "Last year."

"I see," the doctor paused.

"Is everything alright, Doctor?"

"Well, your report shows some abnormalities in one of your breasts. But I need to re-examine to find out the truth," said the doctor.

"What kind of abnormalities, Doctor? Is there anything to worry about?" asked Binita.

"Some kind of Invasive malignant lesions have been detected, but we cannot be sure without a detailed report. I would recommend you to go for a Mammogram urgently," said the Doctor.

"Okay, Doctor. So, can the test be done today?" Binita asked.

"Yes, I will recommend for the urgent test today. Please get

it done. You might have to wait for a while until they are ready. Is it ok?"

"Yes, Doctor!"

"And could you please ask your husband to visit me once you are ready with the report?"

"Yes, Doctor," said Binita.

Right at that time, Surojit called Binita.

He asked, "Is the checkup over? Shall I come and pick you up?"

"Yes, but the doctor has recommended another test, and I may need to wait here for some time and get it done."

"Okay, is everything alright?" asked Surojit.

"I don't know. She didn't tell me anything in detail. She just said that she had found something abnormal in my report and recommended another urgent test. I have to be here for some more time to get the mammogram done, and I am waiting for that," said Binita.

"Okay, I will be right there in a few minutes," said Surojit.

Chapter 17

Surojit was waiting outside when Binita went for her test. A while later, she came out accompanied by a nurse.

The nurse said, "Your report will be ready by noon tomorrow. You can fix an appointment with the reception desk for a consultation with the doctor in the afternoon."

Surojit addressed the nurse and simply said, "Okay."

Then the couple left the hospital, lost in thought.

The next day, Binita and Surojit were at the hospital again, with the doctor. They had given the doctor the reports that they had gotten earlier.

The doctor examined the report and asked Binita, "Did you experience any kind of symptoms before coming for the test?"

"No, nothing in particular. But about 6 months ago, there were some kinds of pustules on my left breast. I had some self-medication and then took a few doses of homoeopathy medicine. After that, there was no problem at all," Binita said.

"So, when the pus formed, did you experience any pain, be it mild or sharp?"

"I used to experience very mild pain for a few seconds occasionally. But after the treatment, there was no pain at all. And in the past 6 months, I did not experience anything anymore. No discomfort, either," said Binita.

"I see," the doctor nodded to herself. "Well, to put it directly without sugarcoating, the report shows that you have breast cancer. And unfortunately, it has just moved from the 2nd stage to the 3rd stage."

She continued after a pause, "Usually, the early stages of breast cancer are symptomless. But it is always recommended that if you experience even mild symptoms in and around the breast area, then you should immediately see a doctor. Frequent breast cancer screening is recommended after the age of 30, and an annual mammogram after the age of 40. If the symptoms are detected early, there are always chances of recovery. But I am surprised that during your last year's annual report, there was nothing. This one seems to have grown so fast."

"What are the chances of recovery, Doctor? Is it too late?" asked Binita, still unable to process the words the doctor was saying. Her heart thudded painfully in her chest.

"No, no! It is never too late. There are always chances of recovery in every stage of life. It depends on how your body responds to that. The faster your mind and body respond to your treatment, the more the chances of healing," the doctor

explained.

"What now, Doctor?" Binita asked, her face clouded with worry.

"Don't worry. We will start with the treatment from tomorrow and see how it progresses. We won't be able to update you on anything else now until we get into the process. Now just relax and go home. You said you have a daughter, right? Spend some quality time with her today, as you need to be in the hospital for the next few days. Get admitted tomorrow at around 7 AM. I will see you at 10 AM. You will be alright soon," said the doctor.

Binita and Surojit drove back home in silence. Both their hearts were filled with sorrow and tension. Surojit could not believe his ears.

Cancer? That too for Binita? NO! It cannot be. God! You cannot do this to me. This is unfair.

Thoughts kept swirling in Surojit's mind as he wondered what was happening.

*****

The next morning, Binita bade goodbye to her parents, in-laws, and her daughter. Everyone was emotional and sad, and they were also speechless.

"Mamma, where are you going?" Titli asked. And her eyes

brimmed with tears.

"I am going to the hospital, baby. I will be back soon. Don't trouble your grandparents while I am away. And finish your homework on time, okay?" said Binita.

*****

Binita was admitted and had settled onto a bed. Surojit was beside her, holding her hands.

In a slow voice, Binita said, "I don't want to die, honey. I want to live and take care of you and our daughter. Please save me."

She started crying softly.

"Nothing will happen to you. You will be fine. Trust me, it is just a matter of a few days. And soon, you will be back home, taking care of us," said Surojit.

Just then, the doctor entered the room. "Good morning, Mrs. Basu. How are you doing today?"

"I am doing alright, Doctor," replied Binita.

The doctor examined her breathing with a stethoscope and said, "You will be alright soon. Now you are in safe hands. So just leave all your worries behind. The rest of the reports are normal and you are doing good on all other fronts. I will see you again in some time."

She then turned to Surojit and said, "Mr. Basu, I would like to meet you in my office."

"Sure Doctor," Surojit said and followed the doctor when she went out of the room. Once they were in her office, the doctor got behind the desk.

"Please have a seat, Mr. Basu. Let me first explain the treatment process. I hope you have insurance coverage?"

"Yes, Doctor," said Surojit.

"That's good. In your wife's case, the best way of treatment is to go for a mastectomy... That way, the cancerous cells from the breast won't get spread to the other organs of the body, and the chances of infection would also be comparatively less. And later on, if there is a need, the breast can be artificially implanted with cosmetic surgery. You can also talk to your wife and let me know your decision at the earliest. We want to get to the surgery as soon as possible."

"Okay, Doctor. Let me discuss the same with Binita and my family. I will confirm and then come and discuss with you in a short while."

"Sure, thank you," said the Doctor.

Chapter 18

Surojit was sitting alone in his bedroom. The room was very dark and he was deep in thoughts that were mired with sorrow.

'My beautiful wife is going to lose one of her organs. I cannot see her like that. No! This should not happen. I cannot see anything artificial on her body. I cannot tolerate that. I cannot face this horrible situation. No! I can't!'

He kept muttering to himself and then held his head in both his palms, feeling pain and anger course through him at the unfairness of it all.

*****

Binita was brought out of the surgery room. She was still unconscious. All of her family members were there – including Surojit and both their parents. Their eyes were on her when the nurses wheeled her stretcher from the Operation Theatre to the private room.

The doctor turned to face everyone and said kindly, "She is doing fine, and will recover consciousness soon. The operation was successful."

After the surgery, her chemotherapy treatment began. She had to stay in the hospital for a long time. She became very weak. She lost weight, and her features changed. She looked very sick and dull all the time, and it got increasingly worse as the treatment progressed. She developed dark circles around her eyes. Her body responded slowly. The doctor was afraid of that and tried all possible alternative means of treatment. Binita mostly remained in the hospital bed, unconscious and immobile. Her parents cried after seeing her condition.

*****

On seeing her mother's condition, Titli hugged her grandmother, Mrs. Basu, and asked, "Grandma! What happened to Mamma? Why doesn't she talk? Why is she not opening her eyes? Tell me, Grandma!"

But Mrs. Basu could not answer the little girl, and she silently cried, trying to console her granddaughter.

No matter how much time had passed, the doctor was not able to discharge her from the hospital, because Binita was on ventilator support.

Binita's hair had to be shaved off during chemotherapy. The changes to her physical appearance were so drastic that Binita looked the opposite of her usual beautiful, graceful self. Her charming countenance had changed.

On the other hand, Surojit remained unmindful and lost in unknown thoughts all the time. He also went around

aimlessly and was careless with his job. Everyone noticed some kind of difference in his behaviour, but no one knew what to do about that. He kept everything inside his mind and never shared his thoughts with anyone. He remained apathetic when it came to taking care of his daughter. The small child now spent all her time with her grandparents instead. Surojit was physically present, but he was so distracted and aimless in his actions that everyone felt his absence.

In the initial days of treatment, Surojit used to visit Binita in the hospital every single day. His day would not begin without seeing her face. He cared for her a lot, too. But with time, he did not care or bother. Sometimes he would visit and sometimes he would refuse to see her. On many days, he would sit alone on the river shore for hours and watch the waves dancing with the lights of the day. He would always be lost to the world in those moments.

He became a loner and would sit in his room alone and ruminate endlessly on something that kept tormenting him. No one would know or read through his face. He always kept his thoughts to himself and never shared them with anyone. He would sometimes think about the good memories he had with Binita, and become happy on seeing her beautiful and soft face. But immediately, reality would intrude, and he would scream by himself on thinking about her horrible face now.

Her bald head and gaunt face terrified him, so he refused to visit her anymore. He got angry, wondering why his wife's beautiful face had been turned into such a shocking state. He did not want to see her again. He questioned himself on why he even married Binita in the first place! Had he not married her, this day would not have come and he need not have suffered like this.

*****

Suddenly, one day, he just disappeared and no one could find him no matter how much they wanted to. His family members left no stone unturned in the search for him but they failed. They also reported his disappearance to the police, hoping that they would get a lead that way. His colleagues did not know his whereabouts either, for he had not come to work in the last few days.

Binita had been wondering what was wrong with him because he had not visited the hospital for a week. She missed her husband and could not even express her feelings to anyone. She had a photo of Surojit and would stare at it often, remembering the early days of her marriage. She would hold the photograph close to her chest and cry like a child.

When she came to know that Surojit was missing and was not to be found anywhere, she was sad and suffered more without expressing her worry and pain to anyone. Her chest swelled in pain, but she had to bear that in silence. She understood that Surojit hated her now because of how gaunt her face had become. She yearned for the earlier relationship she had with her husband, but she was not sure if it would ever come again.

The nurse had to help Binita walk as she could not walk like before because of her weakness. She also took Binita for a ride in her wheelchair in the garden, but Binita looked pale and reacted like a statue. There were no expressions on her face. Titli would sometimes visit the hospital to check on Binita. She would care for her and talk to her about her everyday activities in her innocent style.

Titli would also feed her mother some food with love. Sometimes, she would sleep beside Binita, hugging her tight. Binita would slowly pat her head with her hand that was attached to the saline, ignoring the pain in it. Sometimes, Titli would sit beside her mother and play with her dolls. She would also occasionally bring flower bouquets for her mother and carefully feed her fruit juice with a spoon. Titli would also narrate stories to her mom. Binita would listen to everything patiently, and try to hide her pain. She always pretended to be happy in front of her daughter, just to make her happy. Titli's smiling face always made Binita happy.

*****

Titli once asked Mrs. Basu, "Grandma, where is my father? Is he not going to return home? Does he not love me anymore? Everyone says that my father is lost. Is this true, Grandma?"

Mrs. Basu replied, "No, dear. Your father will come back soon. He has gone in search of God to ask him to help your mother recover. He is devotedly praying to the Almighty God to bring her back to good health as soon as possible."

Titli then said, "Really, grandma? Then I will be waiting for Dad to return with all the prayers and blessings for my mother."

Then she added, "I have become a big girl now. I am 10 years old. I will take care of my mom as she took care of me when I was small. I will make her recover soon. I would feed her, bathe her, sing a lullaby to her and put her to sleep, and do so many other things to comfort her and make her feel good and happy."

Hearing that, her grandmother laughed aloud, wiping her tears. She then hugged Titli and said, "Yes, my dear child. I know you will correct everything. You are our princess and our lucky charm."

Chapter 19

The doctor was discussing Binita's prognosis with Mr. Banerjee.

"Usually, the chances of recovery are higher if the patient's willingness to survive and get through is strong, and they have a strong determination to survive. But Binita's body has not responded positively so far. Her heart rate is getting lower day by day. Strangely, she is deteriorating with time despite the best treatment. Her husband's presence might have helped her with a quicker recovery. Anyway, we are trying our best. For the rest, let us pray to God."

With that, the doctor gently patted Mr Banerjee's shoulder and left the room.

Tears streamed out of Mr Banerjee's eyes. His daughter's body was becoming lifeless in front of his eyes, and he could not do anything about it. Binita slipped into a coma, worsening her state after the treatment. She lay on the bed like a lifeless body for days. Her face looked horrible, with her skin drawn over her bones.

Everything was over now, thought Mr. Banerjee. Nothing was left of his once beautiful daughter, Binita, except her ruined physique.

*****

Even in her comatose state, Binita saw a dream. In that dream, she was talking to her earlier self with a beautiful face.

"What are you doing, Binita? What happened to you? You were never like this before. Why are you ruining yourself now? Why are you lying so helpless in bed? Wake up, Binita. Wake up! I will not let you die. You are the light of your family. You have to live and stand on your own feet. You have to regain your beautiful features. You have to light up your world. If not, so many people would lose their lives in the hands of fate.

"A self-centred person like Surojit cannot hold the power to leave you in this state. I will not let you ruin your life so easily. Surojit only loved your beautiful face. He failed to see that there is a beautiful heart underneath that is immeasurably powerful and ever-lasting. Beauty does not lie only in the external features. There is something deep inside the heart that cannot be seen with our eyes, which can never fade away with the earthly circumstances and bodily decomposition. That something is very raw, divine and truthful. It is priceless.

"You need to show that divinity to the people of this Universe with your presence and deeds. Your job on this Earth is not over, you have a job defined by God. You have to survive this. What would happen to your daughter after you leave? You are born as a human being to fulfil a purpose, and this is the time for it.

"Wake up. Wake up. Wake up, Binita, and see the beautiful morning of tomorrow. It is another new day waiting for you. Another new world awaits you, one which would open the doors of opportunities and success in your life, giving a new meaning to it."

A voice that blended melancholy and hope had whispered all this in her ears and Binita woke up with a jerk. She had regained consciousness with a million thoughts running in her mind. Even though her facial expressions remained blank, her mind had travelled into a new world of enlightenment. She completely forgot that she was in bed and was sick.

Binita also slowly regained her senses. Her limbs were moving. Her heart rate and pulse started improving. Seeing this, the nurse ran to the doctor in excitement.

"Doctor! The patient is responding to treatments. She is conscious now."

The doctor entered the room and when she saw that the patient was recovering, her joy knew no bounds. Binita was trying to open her eyes. The hospital staff quickly informed her family members, and they all came to visit Binita the same day with a heart full of happiness.

The doctor called Mr Basu and Mr Banerjee to her office room and said, "It's a miracle. Without the patient's power of will and intent to survive, this could not have happened. Binita is now back with us due to her desire to live. And there are possibilities of a complete recovery, which is a good sign.

I will monitor her progress for the next 2 days and, based on that, will arrange surgery for breast implants."

The men thanked the doctor emotionally, and Mr Banerjee broke down in tears. The doctor patted his back and left the room. Mr Basu held Mr Bannerjee, hugged him tight and consoled him.

*****

Binita sat up slowly on her hospital bed. Her daughter, mother, and mother-in-law had come to her room to meet her. Her daughter wished her with a fresh bouquet and hugged her tight.

"Mamma, how are you feeling now? We have come here to take you back home!" Titli said.

Mrs. Basu said, "My darling daughter. Let's go home. Without you, our home was not a home at all... it was just a house. We still don't have any news about Surojit. Now you are our only child. You are our son and our daughter."

Chapter 20

Binita's parents came to meet her alone in her room. Binita looked happy and was glowing after a long time. Seeing their tensed face, she asked, "Why are you both still looking sad? Are you still scared of losing me? See, I am recovering well already. I now feel reborn. I am no longer that old Binita. This is my re-birth. I am not going anywhere leaving you all hereafter, so what's the fear now? My time is not over. That's why I am still alive.

"It was the trick of God, who wanted to play with us for a while. He knew that my time was not over and He could not call me back so soon. I will sketch my life in a new way with new chapters. I will give new life to everyone. I will move forward with a new hope. I will get involved in the upliftment of society by working for social causes. I will work towards a better life for humanity diligently. I would bring a huge change in this society with this new lease of life. I will work towards the betterment of people and try to give new homes and families to all orphaned children."

She paused and continued more emotionally, "I will also try to bring back Surojit. You see, he will return someday to all of us because we all love him from the bottom of our hearts. And our inner love and strength would pull him towards us somehow."

Mrs Banerjee heard all this and broke down, crying hard.

Binita tried to console her. "Oh, my goodness! What's wrong with you, Mom? Why are you crying? Did I say anything wrong? Did I hurt you in any way? I am sorry, Mom. I am Sorry!"

Mrs Banerjee nodded and patted Binita's head, wiping the tears from her eyes.

Then Binita said, "See, I am full of energy and happiness. Like any other beautiful day, I can experience the beauty of today. I can see and feel it. These could only be possible with the blessings of God."

*****

Binita's recovery made it easier for the next steps of the treatment to progress quickly after that. The doctors suggested that her breast implant surgery be done quickly.

Binita was still sedated when she was brought out from the Operation Theatre. Her breast implant surgery had been successful. The doctor spoke to everyone as she passed by. "Congratulations! The operation was successful."

After the mandatory recovery period in the hospital, Binita returned home. Everyone pampered her and took good care of her. It felt like all the happiness had returned like a silver lining after a dark cloud that had lingered over them had lifted. Binita's health also improved day by day. Hair had

started growing again on her shaved head. Because of the good post-surgery care, she started regaining her beautiful face and form. Her gaunt face was becoming better and more rounded like before like her deflated cheeks were getting refilled with flesh. She was also getting back to her normal body shape with her limbs and torso fleshing out and fresh blood flowing in. She started looking cheerful and as beautiful as always.

Almost after 8 months of medication and care, Binita started her life afresh with new hope, aspirations, and motivation. After her recovery from the cancer, she decided to change her hairstyle. She cut it short, giving herself a new look with more style and dignity.

*****

Everyone around her could see the difference. Binita was strong, like Goddess Durga. Post the illness and recovery, she started seeing life from a different perspective. She devoted more of her time towards the upliftment of society. She got involved with social work. Her way of executing tasks also changed. She no longer worked for any corporate sector. A more determined confidence rose in her.

Having once fallen on her deathbed and risen from it, she no longer feared death. She wanted to do something bigger and considered that her life's purpose. She visited villages took note of the problems of the women, and put in many efforts to change whatever she could, making many lives better. After her repeated visits, the villagers started breathing with a sigh of relief. They saw various improvements and

developments. They got a dose of new faith and confidence. The fragrance of women's strength and empowerment started floating in the air. Binita helped all the helpless single women to stand on their own legs. She helped them and inspired them through her speeches. She tried to educate them better, too.

For those who lost their husbands, she brought confidence in them with her moral support. She inspired and motivated them to work with her. She guided them along the path of independence and motivated them to start with small cottage industries based on their skills and talents. She taught and facilitated them with different kinds of vocational works like tailoring, handmade art and crafts, pottery, beauty courses, insurance advisory work, clerical office work, pot painting, creating bamboo and cane decorative items, agricultural farming, cooking courses, etc. She also helped open a restaurant run by women, which provided homemade food delivery and services. She helped many women set up their own businesses with low investment.

There was much appreciation for her work in newspapers and news channels, across print and digital media. She had devoted her life to the cause of humanity. She visited all the nearby towns and villages, wherever there was a need for improvement. She donated food, clothing and water to the needy people. She also visited all the slum areas in cities, noted down their problems, and distributed food and other necessities.

She created a Trust using which she expanded the scope of her activities. Her organization also paid for the treatment of poor people. She picked up the girl children who were abandoned by their parents and took them to the appropriate orphanages. She earned a lot of name and fame and also started working in collaboration with international NGOs to give life to helpless women and children over a wider area.

Binita's words and actions inspired the people wherever she went. She also became the beacon of change and betterment. Everyone who heard her life story understood how much she had suffered and gotten through. She was seen as the symbol of power and upliftment.

Chapter 21

Reunion

Suddenly, one day, Surojit returned from nowhere. He came to Binita's office to meet her. The security guard informed Binita, "Someone named Surojit Basu wants to meet you. Shall I ask him to wait?"

Binita was astonished to hear the name after a long time. 'Surojit Basu? Is this my Surojit?' She whispered to her thudding heart.

Her heart became weak for a moment and she got emotional on hearing the name. She was in the middle of work so she requested the guard to make Surojit comfortable in the meeting room. As soon as the security guard left the room, she could not hold herself back. Immediately, she closed the file she was working on and started walking towards the meeting room, feeling anxious and scared. Her throat was dry and she was sweating in tension. She still could not believe her ears.

So many conflicting thoughts started revolving in her mind. Had her husband returned a changed man? She could not wait anymore to see the love of her life.

Surojit's facial features had also changed. The usually clean-shaven Surojit now had a French beard and looked more mature. He looked smarter than before but also more reserved and quieter somehow.

Binita stared at him in silence for a while. The moment her eyes fell on him, she was dumbstruck and her feet froze. Both of them were speechless to see each other. And then, after a while, she suddenly came back to her senses on hearing a noise. She turned her back towards him, held her pain back silently, closed her eyes and asked, "You are here? Where were you all these years? Everyone looked for you everywhere. They all went mad with worry. But you were not found anywhere. No phone calls, no emails, no letters."

She paused, wondering how to phrase the next question that had been tormenting her mind since the day he left. She took a deep breath, worked up her courage, turned around, and demanded, "I know that you hated me. You left me because I was not beautiful anymore, wasn't it?"

Surojit broke down into tears and said, "I have no words left to ask for forgiveness. I have made a huge mistake. I know I have done many things wrong. Please forgive me. I was selfish to think only of myself. I want to return home. I don't dare to face my parents either. But since you are my wife, I came to you first. I want to experience the beautiful life I had lost with you and Titli again. I want to lead our beautiful family life again. You were always the most beautiful woman in this universe, and you are still as beautiful as always."

Binita replied, "Who am I to forgive you? Only parents have

the right to forgive us. They are next to the almighty. I just wanted to let you know that it was not only you who loved me. I have also always loved you from the core of my heart. Did you never think about me even once when you did this? Did you ever wonder what would happen to me without you? You were my entire universe, my life, my love. My world starts with you and ends with you. I could not bear the pain of that separation and my body wanted to take leave from this earthly plane when I heard that you were missing.

"But I am still alive because I had no choice. I promised you once when I conceived our child that if anything happened to either of us, then the other one would stay back to take care of our child. I probably revived only for my daughter. I kept my promise. My love and care for her brought me back to life. I felt as if our little princess was suffering because of our deeds. But she was destined for happiness. What sin had she done at this innocent age that she had to live the life of an orphan? You could disappear without thinking about your daughter, but I couldn't do that. And that's why I am still alive... just to take care of her and her needs. I just extended it to other children of her age who lost their parents for no sin of theirs."

She also added, "Throughout my whole life, I assumed you always thought about others, but I was wrong. I forgot that you mainly think about yourself. You might have done all of these because you thought it was right, and I couldn't understand that. Maybe you were right in your perspective. But my mind refuses to understand the intellectual reality of life. Many things do not get into my head, you know. Maybe I am not smart enough to understand your intellectual mind

that wanted your own good. Maybe I expect too much from you. And that's probably why I suffered a lot."

With a smiling face and tears in her eyes, she faced the stunned and silent Surojit again, "See, I am the happiest woman on this earth because I have already suffered through the punishment that I was destined to face. Maybe I was never right for you. Maybe I am rather selfish, and not you. Maybe I am conservative and narrow-minded. Maybe I am not a perfect human being, and you should rather be praised for leaving us like that. Maybe I am not to be forgiven and you are never even required to ask for forgiveness."

Surojit looked very sad and had paled. "I don't know what to say. Again, I do not have any words to ask for forgiveness. I know you are angry with me, even though you don't express it as much as you should. Binni, I have lived with you for years, and no one understands you better than me. I know you never point out anybody's faults but instead take everything on yourself. I am sorry, Binni. I also suffered like hell without you every second, every minute, and every hour of the day. But sometimes, we cannot show the depth of our internal grief to others. Give me another chance to prove myself and express my true mind. Even if you want my life, I am ready to give you at this moment. I love you, Binni. Please forgive me."

On hearing the pain in his voice, Binita could not utter anything. She could not hold back her tears and ran away from that room, leaving Surojit in a state of guilt and repentance.

The next day, Surojit again came to her office to meet her. She made him sit in her cabin. She did not show any anger this time. Nor she did speak a word. She was busy with her files. Surojit stared at her for hours while she was steadily working.

Eventually, he asked her, "Why are you not talking to me?"

"I got used to living without talking to anybody. So, I don't know what to say. My words are lost. But I am happy to see you beside me. Maybe I don't know who I am now. Maybe my heart is so strong now that it doesn't flutter in love as before. Maybe I became stone-hearted and don't feel for anything," Binita replied

"I am sure that there was nothing special about me, so you didn't feel the need to return earlier. So, I don't blame you for anything. But I am happy that my daughter got her father back, even though it took a long. You could return home and everyone would be happy to see you again. Your parents' precious days have gone in tears without you. But then, hopefully, everything will be alright again once they see that you have returned. You were not there when they needed you. But I am sure they would accept you as always because children cannot be ignored and are always unquestioningly forgiven for their faults by their parents. So, don't be afraid. Go and meet them."

She also added, "I knew you often thought about others. Life is about us, as well. Every individual has come to this earth alone, and no one should expect anything from others. Yes, it was indeed not your responsibility to be by my side at my

weakest. I should not have expected more from you. I am sure that you missed your parents. I knew that you were aware that they were getting old and that they wouldn't be able to handle this pain of separation for long. Your mother spent day after day shedding tears for you.

"I was simply worried about them, wondering what would happen to them. I was also worried that no one would be alive to take care of Titli. What would happen to her if she lost both her parents? She would have become an orphan without us. But I should have known that everyone is strong enough to bear the pain of separation and loss because everything happens for a reason and we just play the role that God has written for us as part of our destiny. God will take care of everyone. Besides, I am sure that you must have done all of this for a good reason. I hope I am right, Surojit?"

"Stop it, Binita! Stop it," said Surojit. "I know you are saying these words out of anger. But I cannot take it anymore. I am feeling guilty about my deeds. Please forgive me. Every time you say good words about me, every time you say that it was not my fault but yours, I feel the pain from within."

Binita then wrapped up her work for the day. She was planning to leave the office and go to pick up Titli from school. She asked Surojit to join her, but he said he had not yet gathered the courage to face his parents.

Chapter 22

Surojit visited Titli's school, but only watched her from a distance. He saw Binita coming to school and picking her up. Surojit yearned to meet his daughter. But he had no courage to face the little girl. What would he reply to his daughter when she asked him about his disappearance? Which father could do such a thing to a daughter? Surojit was struggling and fighting a battle within himself.

Then, randomly, he followed his father from afar. He saw Mr. Basu returning from the market after doing some grocery shopping. Surojit followed him from the market to his house in disguise but didn't dare to stop by him and talk to him, for he would be expected to answer the older man's questions about his disappearance for years.

With a heavy heart, Surojit returned to his hotel room and sat down in deep thought. He had given so much pain to everyone in his family and he had no right to appear and stand in front of them now after all these years. It was his battle and he had to fight it alone.

*****

That night, Binita made Titli's bed and helped her get into it.

"Good night, Mamma," Titli smiled at her.

"Good night, baby," Binita replied, tucking her in.

Then Binita went outside and sat down to have dinner with her in-laws. Over dinner, Binita told both of them, "Surojit came to my office yesterday."

Hearing that, Surojit's mother got excited and asked, "What? Surojit? Where is he now then?" Then she tried to control the warring grief and happiness inside her as she said, "My son is alive. Where is he now? I want to see him. Why he didn't return home?"

Binita didn't reply to anything.

Mrs. Basu asked her again, "Binita, why are you not saying anything? Where is my son? Where had he been all these years? Is he safe and sound? Please say something. I am getting anxious. Please say something!"

Binita replied in a low voice, "I asked him to come home but I don't know what is stopping him. He thinks that he has no right to face any of us. He said he won't be able to answer your questions about his disappearance. He is feeling guilty about everything."

Mrs. Basu said, "What are you saying, Binita? He is your husband. You couldn't bring him back home? You said that you would bring him back someday. But today, when he appeared before you, you simply let him go... Just like that."

Mr Basu intervened angrily. "It is good that he didn't come. He needs to seek permission from me before entering this house. While leaving, he just walked away. But while getting back in, he has to have permission from me after giving me all the valid reasons for disappearing and returning. We don't need him anymore. When there was a need, he was not here. I forgot long ago that I had a son. And I believed that we lost him."

Mr Basu's voice made it clear that he was very angry with his son. He had obviously suppressed the anger at his lost son for years.

He continued shouting, "The man who played with the lives and emotions of so many people has no right to come to my house and show up as if everything is okay now. We have not seen him for years, so we could rather consider that he is dead. We have already learnt to live without him. So, we don't want him back."

"What are you uttering, dear?" Mrs. Basu asked, shocked. "He is our son. And we are his parents. We cannot hold onto our anger like this. Forgiveness is the greatest expression of kindness. There must have been some reason for his disappearance. Maybe he was in such a state that he could not reach out to us all this while. We should listen to his side of the argument before drawing any conclusion."

Mr Basu held up a hand to stop her. "Stop! I do not want to listen to anything in support of him from anybody in this house. If not then, at least now he could have let us know his side of the story. There were many ways to do that. Since he

couldn't do that even now, I do not want to know anything at all from him. This is my last word to all of you. I won't forgive my son for disappearing when my daughter needed him the most. When she was fighting the most horrible battle all alone and was at the most critical phase of her life, he wasn't there.

"Do you not remember what the doctor said to us? Did he not insist that Binita could have recovered fast in the presence of her husband? My daughter suffered like hell because of that man. And from the corner of a father's heart, how can I forgive someone who was the cause of the suffering of my adorable daughter who has been a blessing to us from God? I never taught my son to be inhumane like that. And if he developed that nature in himself then I don't even feel shy to admit that I have not brought him up properly. He has brought disrepute to his name as my son with his deeds. So, enough is enough. There will be no more discussions on this topic in this house."

No one could utter anything after that.

*****

The next morning, Binita stood on her balcony with a coffee cup in hand, enjoying the breeze. The flowers from the flower garden which she could see from there were dancing and swaying in the gentle wind.

Suddenly, her phone rang. It was a call from Surojit. Her phone was on a table inside the room. She came near it and picked it up, but then it got disconnected. She did not ring

him back and put the phone down on the table again.

Surojit called again. And this time, she picked up the call and said, "Hello."

"Binni it is me. Did you get a chance to speak to anyone at home? What is their reaction?" Surojit asked.

She replied, "Nothing."

Surojit asked again, "Binni are you there? Can you hear me?"

"Yes, I am there."

"Why are you so silent, then?"

There was a pause from both ends for a while.

And then Surojit said slowly, "Oh, I understand. Mom and Dad are still angry with me. They have every right to do that. Have you forgiven me, Binni?"

Binita replied, "I was never angry at you."

Surojit replied, "No, Binni I know you are angry. You were not like that before. I do not find my old Binni in you. You seem to have become heartless."

Binita did not reply to any of that and remained silent. She was lost in her thoughts while Surojit was continuously speaking from the other end. She was lost in a world of

happy memories she had enjoyed with Surojit. As a flashback, she remembered a few incidents with Surojit that had made her very emotional and brought a smile to her face along with some tears. She had indeed become stone-hearted out of pain and it was not letting her react normally with her husband. She loved him, no doubt, but his disappearance and her pining love for him hurt her emotions so much that it led her into an unknown world of depression and pushed her into a pit of darkness from where she was not able to come out.

The pain she had gone through was not letting her accept Surojit the way she wanted. This had formed a barrier and created a distance between her heart and Surojit's heart. Binita remained mostly calm and normal all the time. But the moment she met or interacted with Surojit she saw herself becoming a different person, and her body reacted like it was made of stone. Deep in her heart, she was so hurt that she was not able to come out of the self-imposed barrier so easily. She wanted to accept Surojit and wanted to hug him tight, but her emotions were not allowing her that liberty.

*****

One evening, Binita picked up her daughter from the dance class and Titli said, "Mamma, do you know? Today I saw a man at my school. He looked like Daddy. But he was very far from me, so I could not see him properly or identify him. Mamma, did Daddy return? I miss him very much. I want to see him."

Binita replied, "I don't know whether it was your daddy or not, baby. But be very careful before meeting any unknown person, okay? Do not go anywhere outside the premises or near strangers without my permission, okay?"

"Okay Mamma," replied Titli.

*****

Later that night, Binita was on her bed, getting settled in her nightgown. She missed Surojit. She closed her eyes to revisit all the beautiful memories of the days she had spent with Surojit. And in the process, tears rolled down from her eyes. She was experiencing immense pain within her heart, which she could not express to anyone. It felt like she was holding her pain within her and not letting anyone be part of it. She was crying and hugging a pillow close to her heart.

*****

Another evening, when Binita was in her room after returning from her office, Mr. Basu called Binita sounding anxious. There was tension at home. Surojit's mother lay unconscious on the floor in her room. Binita ran into the room. Titli also followed her with a doll in her hand.

Binita was astonished to see the situation. She got closer to her mother-in-law and tried to wake her up touching her slightly with her soft hands and asking, "What happened to you, mom? Wake up!" She patted her cheeks and said, "Open your eyes, Mom!"

She then lifted the glass from the bedside table and sprinkled some water on her face.

Slowly, Mrs. Basu returned to consciousness. Her eyes fluttering open, she muttered, "Suro. My Son, where are you? I want to see you. Please bring him home. Please bring my son home....

Then she slipped back into a faint again.

Binita stood up and turned towards her father-in-law. Mr. Basu also turned towards her but neither of them uttered a single word. It was clear now what went wrong with Mrs Basu.

Titli pulled her mother's dress and asked her, "Mamma. Did Daddy return? Where is he now? Why was Grandma uttering his name again and again?"

Mrs. Basu was still on her bed. She was conscious again but did not move much. She was muttering Surojit's name in her sleep.

Mr Basu immediately called a doctor and said, "Dr Sen, this is Omolendu Basu. My wife is lying unconscious on her bed."

Then, after a pause, he again replied, "She regained consciousness, but is only partially conscious. Could you please come and see her once?"

There was a short burst of talk at the other end and Mr. Basu

said, "Thank you. Thank you, Doctor."

Binita and Mr. Basu held Mrs. Basu and made her sit erect on her bed. Her shoulders were slightly bent on one side. She was still half-conscious and was not able to open her eyes properly. Her words were not clear.

Titli held her grandmother tight and placed her head on Mrs Basu's chest. Then she asked, "What happened to you, grandma? Open your eyes. See, my doll and I are waiting to listen to your stories. Why are you not speaking to me now? Do you wish to see Daddy? Why are you muttering his name?"

Mrs. Basu could not speak, but tears rolled down from her eyes. Then she patted Titli's head, slowly uttering the words, "I am alright. I just miss my son. Did your daddy return? I want to see him."

Titli replied out of excitement, "Really, grandma? Has Daddy returned?"

Binita then addressed Titli. "Come here, baby. Let grandma get some rest. I will answer all your questions."

Titli came to Binita and asked her, "Mummy, is this true? Did Daddy return? But I didn't see him. Where is he, Mummy?"

The doorbell rang. Dr Sen had arrived. Mr. Basu received him and brought him to where Mrs. Basu was sitting up.

After diagnosis, the doctor said, "There is nothing to worry about. Her BP is on the higher side. The pulse rate has also reduced. I think she went through some kind of stress. Was she going through anything of that sort?"

Mr. Basu replied, "Yes, our son was not at home all these days. She has not seen him for years. This is probably because of that."

"Oh, I see. No worries. She will be alright. Just see to it that she is being taken care of properly. Allow her to take as much rest as possible. And keep checking her pulse rate every hour."

"Sure, doctor," replied Mr Basu.

The doctor also added, "If you notice any kind of abnormalities, then immediately call an ambulance. I am writing a medicine for her to sleep properly tonight. It would relax her nerves. She might sleep for long because of the medication. But don't get nervous. Update me once tomorrow morning."

"Thank you, Doctor. Sorry to have bothered you urgently at this hour," said Mr. Basu.

"No, no! Not at all. I was anyway on my way back home. There was no trouble at all."

Binita also thanked the doctor. She then took the mobile and tried reaching Surojit. "Hello, could you come home immediately?" she asked. "Mom is unwell. She is half conscious and is repeatedly muttering your name only. She desperately wants to see you. Can you come right away?"

"Yes, yes. I will be right there in a few moments," said Surojit.

"Okay. Please get medicines for her on your way. I will text you the prescriptions," said Binita.

"Sure, I will, replied Surojit.

Mr Basu sat next to his wife and started patting her head consolingly.

Meanwhile, Binita said to Titli, "Baby, let's go to your room. Let Grandma and Grandpa take some rest."

"Good night, grandpa," said Titli, and they took a leave from that room.

Chapter 23

The doorbell rang. Mr Basu opened the door. Surojit was waiting anxiously on the other side. Mr Basu stared at Surojit for a while without uttering a word and then silently stepped back to let him come inside.

Surojit went to his mother's room. Mrs. Basu was tossing and turning on the bed. Surojit went near her and patted her head slowly. She turned around, opened her eyes, and saw Surojit. Out of excitement, she tried to sit up straight. Surojit helped her to sit and gently held her shoulders.

Mrs. Basu hugged him tight. She started crying loudly, "Where were you, my son? I missed you so much. I thought I would never see you again before I die. I lost all hope after waiting for you all these years. I held back my tears and emotions in my heart without letting anyone know what I felt in your absence. I was dying from within."

Surojit did not say anything because he had no words. But he hugged his mom tight, placed his head on her shoulder, and closed his eyes. He was also experiencing pain and joy within himself.

Mr Basu was seated in a chair with his head bent. Surojit then walked towards his father and greeted him by bowing down

and touching his feet. Mr. Basu did not utter a word. But though his face was turned to the other side, he blessed Surojit with his hands. Surojit handed over the medicines he had bought to his father.

Mr Basu then gestured at Surojit to sit next to his mother. He took the medicine and walked out to hand them over to Binita. Binita put Titli to sleep and came out of the room.

Mr. Basu said, "Surojit arrived. And here are the medicines."

Binita brought some water and the medicines to Mrs. Basu's room. She did not look at Surojit even once. She tried to avoid looking at his eyes. And then she fed medicine to her mother-in-law silently. Surojit kept on staring at Binita for a while.

Mrs. Basu then addressed her son. "Don't ever leave me again, son... Don't act insane. I won't survive for long if I don't see you. Go and take some rest now, and don't leave the house. Binita will make your bed."

Saying this, she patted her son. Surojit nodded to her and covered her with a blanket. He then touched her feet to take her blessings and left the room.

The next morning, Titli woke up and asked her mother, "Mamma did daddy arrive?"

Binita kissed Titli's forehead and said, "Yes, your daddy is in the room next to your grandma's room. Go and see him."

Titli jumped from her bed holding a doll in her hand and ran to her father's room. Surojit was lying awake on his bed. Titli knocked at the door and then entered. She ran towards her father, yelling, "Daddy!" She then hugged him and jumped onto his bed. Both father and daughter hugged each other tight.

Surojit kissed her with fatherly affection. He got very emotional as he held his daughter in his lap and tears started rolling down his cheeks. Binita was watching them from behind a curtain, and she got very emotional, too. She too felt like hugging him tight. She was happy to see the bond between the father and the daughter after almost two years. She knew how much her daughter missed her father.

Surojit held Titli tight. He looked at her with so much love and affection. He promised himself to never leave this family again.

*****

Mrs Basu had fully recovered after seeing her son. The very next day, she could sit up by herself on the bed and even walk short distances. Her blood pressure had also come to normal limits. She also had a good sleep after taking medication. In the morning, she woke up, stood on her feet, and went to meet her son in his room. She sat beside him and listened to his stories patiently and also shared everything that happened all these years in his absence.

On the other hand, while mother and son were busy, Titli got ready for her school. She said goodbye to her father and

grandparents. She went to her father's room and said, "Bye, Daddy. I have lots of stories to share with you after school. So, don't leave the house, okay?"

She then kissed Surojit on his cheeks and turned to her grandmother. "Grandma, you spend all the time you need with your son today while I am away at school. I will come in the evening, and again take him away from you. Bye, grandma."

Mrs. Basu also said goodbye to her. Binita drove the car and dropped Titli at school.

*****

Later that day, Surojit again went to Binita's office. The security informed Binita that Surojit was again waiting to meet her. She asked the security to send Surojit to her cabin.

Seeing Surojit, she immediately asked, "What's wrong? Why are you here? Is Mom doing alright?"

Surojit replied, "Yes, she is doing fine. I just felt like meeting you. This morning, you were busy with Titli. I couldn't talk to you much. So I thought of coming here. You carry on with your work. I won't bother you here. I will just sit next to you and watch you work. And then, we both can go to pick up Titli together from her school."

Throughout the day, he sat next to Binita, just staring at her. They didn't talk to each other much and did not bother each

other. Sometimes, Binita stared at him when Surojit was busy looking elsewhere.

Then, just before leaving the office to pick up Titli, he said, "Binita! Wait for a minute. I want to say something."

Binita stopped, looked at him and asked, "What?"

"Please give me a chance. I want to atone for my sins. Please talk to me like before. I want to see the Binita I loved. You seem to have changed a lot and I know the reason behind it. I know I am to blame. I hurt you so hard that now your soft heart has turned to stone. I cannot see you like this. I want to talk to you the whole day. I want to give you all the love that you deserved from me all these years, which I failed to give you. I want to fill your life with love and joy again. More love than ever before. Give me a chance again. I love you. I love you, Binni. I know you love me too and want to hold me like before. But then, you are stopping yourself.

"Why are you hurting yourself, Binni? I cannot see you getting hurt like this anymore. Let me know what I should do for you. You do not deserve to be punished anymore. If anyone has to suffer, then it should be me. But not you anymore, honey."

Binita did not give any reaction to his passionate words. She listened to everything patiently but did not utter any word or show any anger.

She then started arranging her files in order and was getting ready to leave the room. When she was about to walk out,

Surojit stopped her. He asked her to reply and say something before walking out. But she didn't answer his question. Instead, she said, "I don't know what to say, and I don't have any answer to your question."

She then started heading towards the door.

Surojit again stopped her by holding her hands tight. Binita was moved by his touch after many years. She could feel herself getting emotional. She said in a low tone, "Let go, it's hurting."

Surojit replied, "I won't. Not until you say yes."

Binita asked, "Yes to what?"

"That you have forgiven me and will accept me the way you used to before," said Surojit.

Binita replied, "I never said that I am angry with you. I still love you. And no matter how much people try, they cannot be angry with their loved ones."

"Ask yourself the question and be truthful to yourself! I don't think so," said Surojit. "If it is true, then why are you not the same to me as you were before? Why are you behaving like this with me? Why am I not getting any positive vibes from you? Why can't I see and feel the love that I always saw in your eyes? I need an answer today. Right at this moment."

Binita tried to release her wrist. But Surojit pulled her

towards him, brought her close to his chest and made her feel his breath.

Binita felt emotional, nervous and tense. Her heart was beating fast. She was getting weak. Surojit then silently released her. She ran and got into the car and waited for him.

Chapter 24

Binita and Surojit were on a rooftop balcony/garden. They stood in two opposite directions with their backs turned to each other.

Surojit broke the silence. "I love you very much, Binni. This distance between us is hurting me. Do you want me to prove my love to you? Shall I commit suicide now? If dying for you can prove my love for you, then I am ready to do that right away. Just command me! Tell me what I need to do. I cannot stay far away from you like this.

"You wanted to know where I was all these years, right? Then let me tell you the truth. I was lost for a moment when the doctor said that anything could happen to you. I was a coward and was scared to face the fear of your loss. When I saw your skeletal body, I lost control of my mind and body. I was terrified of losing you. I lost every hope. I got weak and nervous. I felt like I had lost everything and there was nothing left to survive. Everything was over. I never thought of a life without you. I could see darkness surrounding me. I lost any hope of surviving.

"I never thought even in my nightmares that a day might come when I might have to live without you, because I was not mentally prepared for that. Everything happened so suddenly that I could not even think of it. I wanted to end my

life before you left this earth. That day, I thought I should rather kill myself before anything of that sort happened to you because my ears wouldn't be able to take that news.

"My brain collapsed. I could not see anybody else other than you. I could only hear your voice. I could not see Titli, my mother, and my father. You were everywhere around me. I was not able to decide what was I supposed to do. My whole body was numb and paralysed.

"Then, one day, early in the morning, when it was very dark outside and everyone was sleeping, I decided to leave home and go to the Ganges. I walked towards the shore and then to the middle of the river so I could drown myself. I held my breath for as long as I could so that I would stop breathing and give my life to Mother Ganga. I felt unconscious and after that, I don't know what happened or how I got to the other shore again.

"When I came back to my senses, I found myself amongst a group of fishermen in a village. I did not disclose my identity to them. During my short stay in that village, I happened to meet a Buddhist Monk one day. I started following his preachings with his other followers. His preachings helped me to temporarily come out of my pain and grief, and I shared my problems with the monk himself. He showed me the path of enlightenment and helped me to come out of my darkness and the feeling of distress. I followed him to the Ladakh Thiksey monastery and started following his preachings there. I was there all these years under the umbrella of Lord Buddha.

"I never tried to contact you back home, because I was afraid of hearing the horrible news about you. Believe me, I was there only, all these years. I could never find me in myself. I was lost in a different world. I was alive, but I felt as if my soul was not in my body. I was lifeless. It was as if no emotions around me could move or shatter me. I could see only the dark world. I could neither feel my pain nor the life within me. I was dead with a living, breathing body. And sometimes, I lived without even eating for days because I never felt like eating. I had no appetite or thirst. I was like a dead soul that needed no nourishment for life.

"Suddenly, one day, your name struck my ear. I heard people uttering your name even in Ladakh. Your name brought life and sense to my soulless body. And I started behaving like a human again. After that, I started scouring more information about you. I got to see you in a news video someday. And then I could not stop myself. I came running to you. I cannot explain to you how happy I was to see you alive and thriving again.

"I felt like I lost nothing, and whatever had happened was just a nightmare. But now your distance from me hurts me. It is dragging me back to the dark corner where I remained soulless all these years. My life started with you and will end with you. Do not get me wrong. I really love you. I do not have anyone else but you. And I do not want anything else in life other than you. I love you and I will always love you until my last breath; even after that. You are the light of my life and even after death you would be my light."

Both of them got emotional after that.

Binita said in a low soft voice, "I am sorry. I am really very sorry. I am not worth the depth of your love."

She put her head down in shame.

Surojit held her shoulder with both his hands and said, "No, no! No, Binni. Don't say that. It is not your fault. You have every right to punish me."

Then Binita cried as she spoke.

"And what if you leave us again someday? What will happen to me then? I will die again without you. I stood up once, but I might not stand up again and again. I was also dead and soulless without you! Did you know how I felt when I could not see you in the hospital anymore? We promised each other that we would always live together. When I could not hear your voice anymore, I gave up hope. I never wanted to recover. I wondered what's the use of a life without you. It was better to be dead than alive without you. I felt like voluntarily lay on the lap of death because dying would be much more painless than bearing the pain of your loss.

"Did you know what was my state of mind then? Only by seeing the face of our daughter did I experience the light of life again. And then I recovered. And, to give new life to the helpless children of society, I came back to life. I also came back for the helpless women of society. If God had not given me a purpose that day, I would not have been alive today, in front of you."

Surojit said, "I also want to work for the social welfare of the people, Binni. Give me one chance, please. We will again start everything afresh. I do not want anything else. You are beside me, and I have my whole world."

Then they hugged each other and cried on each other's shoulders. They felt peace in their heart after sharing their pain. Surojit then took out a case of vermillion from his pocket.

Binita had not worn vermillion in the intervening years, because she thought that something might have happened to her husband.

But now Surojit applied Vermillion on the parting of her hair. Then he took out another case from his pocket that held a diamond ring. He took out the ring, put it on her finger and wished her, "Happy Wedding Anniversary to us. It is midnight now. Today is our 14th wedding anniversary."

Both of them laughed aloud in happiness and again hugged each other tight in emotion.

*****

Everything was perfect again. Binita forgave Surojit and accepted him. And hence, Mr Basu also accepted his son again.

Surojit greeted everyone by touching their feet. The lost son of the house had returned. Titli got into her father's lap. Then there was a family photo session. Binita's parents were also there in the picture. And they happily blessed the couple with their love and prayers. And they all lived happily ever after.

THE END

Author Biography

Born in a Bengali family, Pompi Mazumdar originally hails from the Cachar District, Assam, India. She grew up in a beautiful little town named Silchar, Assam. After completing her post-graduation (MBA in Human Resource Management & Marketing Management), in the year 2006, Pompi moved to the city of Bangalore, Karnataka, where she worked for various multi-national companies as a human resource professional.

Pompi is a very ambitious, self-motivated, and committed person, who thrives on the passion to create, especially through her writings in multiple languages, such as English, Hindi, and Bengali. Among her other interests in life is her intense love for art, culture, music, poetry, photography, and interior decoration. One could also consider her to be a travel junkie, with a passion for everything travel: places, regional cuisines, novel cultures, and, well, adventure sports.

Besides being a novelist, Pompi is a blogger for various websites including WordPress.Com, Momspresso.Com, and JobsForHer.Com, where she experiments with her writing across various genres on various subjects, topics, and styles. She is also a poet, having written over 100 poems in Hindi (in original Hindi and Roman scripts). But Pompi's love for literature transcends writing, and she is an avid reader who enjoys exploring the writings of different authors.

Presently, Pompi resides in the United States Of America with her family and works as a professional for a well-known retail industry.

She also scripted,directed and produced a women centric Youtube series (GUPSHAP). The series is by mothers and is for women empowerment. It is about the culture of Indians in America. 15 episodes have already been released so far. Few more episodes of the Gupshap series are yet to come in the next few weeks.

GUPSHAP series can also be found on her Youtube channel " Pompi Mazumdar I United States Of America".

Browse on to her channel and click the video tab to find all the released episodes of Gupshap.

Pompi is also a blogger and her blogs can be read at

http://www.pompimazumdar.wordpress.com/blog/.

Given below are her published works:

Steps to Gain Success In Life & Career

Tale of Five Families

Discovering & Untying Multiple Shades

36 Short Stories

Sparsh: Poetry Book (A Collection of 100 + 3 Poems in English-Hindi-Roman Script)

Divya Drishti (Poetry Book): (Man ka Darpan): A Collection of 103 Poems in Hindi Script (Hindi Edition)

The Black Fear: A Short Murder Mystery Novel

Melodrama: A Murder Mystery

Children's Alphabet Book with 1500 + Words & 1000 + Exciting Pictures: For Beginners

Quick Cooking Recipes for Working Women, Busy Mothers and Non-Cooking Lovers

Modern Bengali Poetry (Book of Poems in Bengali but in English letters)

Holy Wings Of Love(Light after darkness) Book of Poems in English

Explore The Unexplored: The Travellers Guide To Nevada, United States Of America

All the above books are available at

www.amazon.in

www.amazon.com

www.notionpress.com

Contents